"I dreamed about you last night, Troy. Can you guess what I dreamed?" I lean toward this good-looking guy and put my other hand on his arm.

"What?" he asks. His face gets a caved-in look. His lips part. His eyes are fastened on mine.

"That you kissed me," I say softly.

Troy comes closer. He lifts my arms and puts them around his neck. "I don't know about dreams. They don't have much to do with real life. But that one, that's one dream we can make come true." He lowers his face.

I notice his nose. It is round on the end, not pointed like Kyle's. He is so close his nose touches my cheek.

Then Troy kisses me. . . .

Also by Charlotte St. John
Published by Fawcett Juniper Books:

RED HAIR

RED HAIR, TOO

Charlotte St. John

FAWCETT JUNIPER • NEW YORK

This book was written for Claire,
my sister

CHAPTER ONE
Emily

Two guys are on the floor looking at a Michael Jackson book. They stop at the pictures and laugh like hyenas. A girl standing over them swivels her hips and strums an imaginary guitar. She belts out a line from an old Mick Jagger song and monkey-shuffles down the aisle.

Nobody pays any attention to me. These kids act like I'm not here.

I look at the teacher, who happens to be my mother. Can she handle this crazy bunch?

My mother is a social worker and this is her group of first offenders.

Mama leans over the front row to talk to a couple of her "students." She is helping them work out some action lines for a one-act play.

They whisper. My mother raises her head and signals to a guy sitting in front of me.

"Troy," she says, "we want you to play the guy's part."

Troy gets to his feet. The way he stands one shoulder is slightly higher than the other. The same with his behind. He leans against the chair and shakes his head.

"I don't know what to do in that part. What is the guy supposed to do?" he asks.

"Tell him, class," Mama says, turning to the rest of us. Before these jailbirds can work themselves up into a roar, she wriggles her fingers and says, "One at a time. Ellie, why don't you review the scene for us? Tell Troy what is supposed to happen here."

A girl sitting behind me says, "They're arguing. The guy and the girl are mad at each other."

My mother nods and points to a kid in the second row.

This guy puts out his hands like he is patting the air and says, "The girl went out with another guy. She didn't want her guy to find out . . . but he did. He starts to blast her for it but she takes over. She blasts him. Why is she mad? The guy is the one who should be mad."

"Aha!" My mother's big eyes get bigger. "Why does this girl act like the injured party? Who can tell us?"

"Me, me!"

I turn around. There is this thin, stiff black girl sitting two seats behind me twirling her hand in the air. Mama nods at her.

"Because . . . because she is trying to cover up. She is going to con the guy. She wants to mess up his head real good. If she can confuse him, he won't fuss at her."

My mother sits up in her chair and narrows her eyes at the black girl.

"Come up here, Maya. You are going to do the girl's part."

Maya walks up to the front. Troy follows, slowly. He turns around and faces the class. This is the first time I have seen his face. He is Mexican like my mother.

He looks nervous. I can't see why. This is the kind of play you can make up as you go along. But this dude's hands are making fists in his pockets. If he would relax, he would be good-looking. His skin is creamy. There is nothing wrong with his eyes, either. Slitted and fiery. They simmer even when he smiles. Which he is doing now. At me!

This guy is staring at me. He looks surprised. Am I so surprising? I look away. In a minute, I look back. He is still staring. Hasn't he ever seen a redheaded woman before?

The black girl, Maya, says something to him and he looks at her. "Uh, what do we do first?" he asks stiffly.

Mama tosses her long hair. "This isn't a movie studio," she says. She flings out one of her small hands, all fingers twitching. "Just start. You are having this argument. Make it up as you go along."

Troy and Maya begin to argue. They don't sound convincing. I look around, beginning to get bored. Then I remember where I am.

* * *

When I came out here to California from Florida to visit my mother and my twin sister, I never dreamed I would be sitting in a class with kids who shoplift, sell drugs, and mug people on the streets. Okay, so they have done these things only once. Or at least been caught only once. That is what "first offender" means, as my mother explained. As a social worker, she deals with all kinds. But I don't understand how she can be so casual about it.

As a judge, my father works with all kinds, too, but he is not so easygoing. My parents are very different. That's why they got divorced soon after I was born.

This morning when Mama and I were crossing the Golden Gate Bridge, I watched her whiz through traffic that would have made my dad's hair stand on end. In and out, swerve left, change lanes, hurtle through space. I looked way, way down out of the car window. Way down there was the sun rising over the shimmering bay. Scary? To me, yes. But, judging from the way she was driving, my mother is totally fearless. Also she was a little bit late.

She lives in Corte Madera, across the bay from San Francisco where she works.

I glanced over at her. All she does in the morning is pull a dress over her head and run a comb through her hair. And looks gorgeous.

She glanced at me. Immediately, I felt uncomfortable. I didn't want to come to this class this morning.

"Elaine has been to this drama class with me

several times. You can't let your twin get ahead of you, Emily. Besides, this will be good for you. You need to broaden your experiences with people. Where you grew up everybody knew who everybody was. You were the girl who lived in the biggest house in town." She half closed her eyes and smiled teasingly at me. "Here, you are just another pretty face."

I have been teased about my big house all my life. But with Mama it's different. With her it isn't envy. My mother doesn't want to live in a big house.

"Why are you teaching these kids how to act? They aren't going to be actors when they get out, are they?" I could have bitten my tongue. My mother doesn't like references about being "in" or "out" of jail where her precious students are concerned.

"They aren't in jail, you know. They are in Juvenile Hall. Quite a different matter." She watched the road. "I am not teaching them to be actors. This morning I am going to help them act out some of their problems. I want you to understand that their problems are very much like anybody else's problems. Like yours and mine. Of course there are differences. They didn't grow up like us. As differently as you twins were raised, you both grew up in safe homes. You can't imagine what some of these kids have been through. . . ."

"Give me a break, Mama."

My mother swung her head toward me, surprised.

"I've seen it all," I insisted. "I've seen dozens of those kinds of kids." It was true. Back home I visited my father's court any time I wanted to.

Thinking about my father made me homesick. I smoothed the scarf around my neck. It shimmered like the bay. It is an old scarf, made of silky, rainbow colors. Dad gave it to me just before I left. I was touched. I know it was one of his special treasures. My dad and I are very close.

Slowly, my mother says, "I see." We were silent for a few minutes. We weren't really mad at each other. I haven't known my natural mother very long, but already I have found out that we can disagree and still be friends.

My twin, Elaine, and I were babies when our parents were divorced, and we have been separated nearly all of our lives. Elaine grew up on the West Coast with our mother. I grew up in Fern, Florida with Dad and my stepmother. My dad, my stepmother, and I thought my real mother and my sister were dead. Then, out of the blue, Mama and Elaine came to Florida last summer. I nearly died of excitement. Everything seemed wonderful. It still seems wonderful, but it is more like a dream than reality. The question is: will life ever feel normal again?

I don't want to go back to a time when I didn't have my mother and my sister. I just want to wake up some morning feeling normal instead of upside-down. That's one reason I came for this visit during my fall break from school . . . to try to "adjust," as they say.

We were across the bridge. A few blocks into town my mother pulled up in front of the Rehabilitation Center and parked the car. Neither one of us made a move to get out.

"I can see that you have some experience with the criminal justice system. It's just that . . . well, I want you to give these kids a chance. Try not to think of them as 'those others.' Think of them as 'us.' Okay?" Carefully, she opened her door and stepped out of the car.

What did she mean? They aren't like me. I would never steal. My friends wouldn't either. I mean, I've seen kids who do. I have seen them face my father as their lawyers plead for them. I've seen lots of these kids loaded into vans to be taken off to Juvenile Hall. Of course, I've never known any of them personally.

We were walking toward the Rehabilitation Center when Mama said, "The kids you are going to see in a few minutes are real achievers. They make your straight-A high-school student look slow. In a few months they have learned more than most kids learn in a year of high school."

I gave her a short nod that could mean anything.

We reached my mother's precious class. The noise came through the walls. We went in and I headed for the back. Now, twenty minutes later, I am watching Troy and Maya "act out some of their problems."

* * *

Mama is right about this guy, Troy. No question, Troy has learned some things. Such as how to make a girl feel sexy. Just looking at him makes me get ideas.

I am looking at Troy when I realize that the action isn't boring anymore. It is beginning to sound like a real argument. Troy is backing up, hands in the air.

What strikes me is that this muscular guy looks . . . so defenseless. Like he could use some help. As Maya bears down on him, she shows her teeth in a snarl. For a second, I think Troy is going to make a dash for his seat. He doesn't like this kind of action any better than I do. He is overwhelmed. I can relate to that!

My guy back home, Kyle, was never overwhelmed. There is nothing I could say that would make him back up one inch. Kyle is almost too independent.

I don't get to think about Kyle very long because somebody starts yelling. It is Maya.

Now I'm watching Maya. What happened to her? Did I say she was stiff ? She isn't now. She is scooting around Troy waving her arms and screaming. I have to remind myself she is just acting out a part, but she seems so furious it feels to me as though she isn't acting at all. This kid is scary.

Everyone around me is loving it. Ellie, the girl behind me, stands up and shouts, "Go, Maya, go!" I want to put my fingers in my ears.

But that would attract attention. I look down and concentrate on my feet.

The screaming stops. The scene is over. Maya and Troy go back to their seats and I breathe a sigh of relief.

My mother dismisses the class and there is a mad scramble for the door. I stay where I am to avoid being trampled. I am still studying my feet when two other feet sidle up beside mine. Someone is standing near my chair. I look up.

Troy!

"What are you doing here? Didn't you say you weren't coming back for a couple of weeks?" he asks.

He must think I am Elaine. If I let him think it, I won't have to explain who I am. I am wondering how to play it when he says, "What do you think? How did I do up there?" He points toward the front of the room. He means was his acting okay.

"Great. You were great," I say. We Southerners are programmed to compliment.

The guy looks puzzled. He sits in the chair beside me.

"You really think so?" he asks. He makes it sound like the most important question in the world. "You amaze me, Elaine. Last week you think I stink. This week you think I am great?" He pauses. "And another thing, why are you talking funny?"

I laugh. He has mixed me up with my twin, and it would be fun to go along, but something tells me I want this guy to know who I am.

I put my hand against my chest.

"I am Emily. Elaine is my twin sister," I say.

Troy draws back. Slowly, he points a finger at me. He scowls. Then he smiles. "Elaine told me about you. Talk about identical! Except for your accent. How do you two remember which one you are?" He stops, suddenly surprised. "But you are different, too. There is something about you. I couldn't figure it out. That's why I had to stare." He studies my face. "Now that I know, I can see . . . how different you are."

"My father says he can tell Elaine and me apart because Elaine is the sassy one," I say. To myself I admit that Dad's saying this annoys me. He makes "sassy" sound adorable.

"Yeah. That fits, all right." He hesitates. "Sassy is okay but there are better things. In my humble opinion."

My heart gives a bounce. Is the guy telling me he likes me better than my twin?

"Like what?" I ask. I am not usually so pushy. Especially with a new guy. But it wouldn't break my heart if he were to elaborate on the subject.

Again, Troy hesitates. Maybe he doesn't want to come out and say it, but his eyes are telling me before he opens his mouth.

"I don't know. Maybe I just like the things you say. You are easy on a guy, you know that?" he says. He rears back and shakes his head. "I'm getting off to a bad start here. I didn't mean to sound like I didn't like your twin. Elaine is a cool character. Nothing bothers her. In fact, she can get as noisy as the rest of us. That's why I was surprised when I saw her ... I mean you ... looking like you were about to jump out of your skin. When the action heated up, I thought you were going to get up and run out of the room."

"I didn't know it showed," I say.

"Don't worry about it. It's not you. It's this place. It's these kids. I mean, I like them all right. But some of the guys dropped out of school two or three years ago. To them, every place is a place to hang out."

Is Troy telling me he is different, too? Is he saying that, like me, he is not like the other kids in here? Suddenly, I am in no hurry to leave. Troy starts to say something else but Mama calls him.

"Time to go, Troy, dear," she says. The kids are going outside to the bus that will take them back to Juvenile Hall.

It is hard to believe Troy is one of them. That he has committed some kind of crime. That he can't live at home with his family. That, just like all the other kids here, he has to be kept away from society until people like my mother think he is ready to live around the rest of us again.

"Be right there, Evita," he says to Mama while looking at me. His eyes are not slits now, they are open wide. I can see the little gold flecks in the brown. That makes them warm brown, doesn't it? To me he says, "I won't think you are your twin next time. You are coming back to class, aren't you? This acting thing is not for me, but it's fun to watch."

"I might come back."

"Does that mean you'll be here tomorrow?" he asks.

"Do you want me to?" I hold my breath. I need to hear him say it.

He looks away. Does he have to think it over? He looks back. "Sure." He shrugs his shoulders.

"I mean if you want me to come back, I will," I say. I wish I didn't sound so anxious.

"Sure, of course I do." He says it too fast.

The guy stands there looking at me. A funny look. I can't read it.

But he said what I wanted to hear!

"I promise," I say. "I'll be here tomorrow. Let's get together early so we can talk some more, okay?"

"Whatever you say." He nods a couple of times.

I looked into his eyes. Like me, Troy, I command silently. Please like me. I keep looking. I add a special smile and his whole face seems to soften. A surge of hope rises from my toes and hits the top of my head. Could I make this guy fall in love with me?

Troy walks to the door. He looks back once before he goes out.

I help my mother gather up her books.

"Cute, isn't he?" she says.

Cute? There's got to be a better word than cute. How about devastating?

In a very ordinary voice, I ask, "What did he do? I mean how come he's here?"

"Nothing terrible. Actually, we aren't supposed to tell. None of these kids is a crook, you know. By the way, what did you think of the class?"

"It's great."

"Did you really think so?"

No. But I don't want to hurt this short, pretty Mexican woman that I have known only a couple of months. She stops at the door and looks at me. I've had those looks before. From my stepmother. Both my mothers can read my mind.

"You are a polite child, Emily. But you can level with me. I won't evaporate if you tell me what you really think."

Suddenly, I know I can tell her.

"Your precious kids are weird. That Maya— did she have to scream and throw things? I know she was just acting, but it was too much." I shudder and Mama puts an arm around me. "Then there were those other kids. Did you know two guys in the back of the room were punching each other out over a quarter they found on the floor? I mean, they weren't really fighting, but why do they act like such babies?"

We are walking toward the door. Mama stops and puts her books down on a chair. She hugs me, hard.

"My Emily," she murmurs.

How can I feel so close to this stranger? This new feeling, this sweet closeness, it hits me in the pit of my stomach. I am taller than my mother so I have to bend down to snuggle into her arms.

"It must be hard for you, this whole deal. California. Elaine. Me. It's a big change and it's going to take some getting used to."

I want to tell her about Troy, how I feel about this new guy. Because I feel something special for him.

"I thought Troy was terrific," I say.

She pushes me away and studies me. "Oh. That's funny. Troy is a whiz at math. He helps in the office. He keeps the books. But here . . . he doesn't respond. Like today. Did you notice? He didn't defend himself. That is a problem for Troy. He gives up too easily. Actually, it was Maya that grabbed my attention." She thinks about it. "Ah, well, I suppose it is only natural for a young woman like you to take notice of a handsome fellow like Troy."

I give her a sharp look.

"I'm only joking. I know you aren't really interested in Troy. Not as long as you've got your guy back home, right?" She smiles and we go outside. "By the way, have you heard from Kyle lately?"

"Kyle rhymes with bile. Hey, I just thought of that!" I am laughing. Mama looks at me, soberly. "Yeah, I've heard from him. And I'll write him soon." If she must know.

Cheerful again, she starts humming in her throat.

This Mexican, she likes country and western

songs. Now she sings a few lines. The words coming out of her mouth seem ridiculous to me. Something about a country boy. How he can survive. I wish she liked a different kind of music, something that suited her better. Like that stuff Linda Ronstadt sings, for example. Something for Latin women. And let's face it, something for older women.

Compared to this natural mother of mine, my stepmother is a little prim and proper, but she never did anything to embarrass me. Not that Mama embarrasses me, exactly. I am very proud of Mama. I am especially proud of being half Mexican, thanks to her. But she could change a little bit and be even better. I try to think just what I mean as I watch her walking in front of me. Such little steps. Such little feet. A short, curvy body in free-swinging clothes. Deep, strong colors. All that black hair she wears like a girl, hanging down her back.

Am I complaining? How could I be? I feel a pang of guilt. My mother is gorgeous I tell myself for the one hundredth time. I am in love with her Mexican ways. The crazy food, so hot I have to drink tons of water after eating it. The talk . . . the mixed-up languages. Half the time to my mother, I am *querida mia*, which translates into something like "my much-loved little girl." But I am glad the kids back home aren't listening to her right now. She has changed tunes and is singing a real hicky oldie. Her voice is low and it has an alto twang to it. It carries to every corner of the parking lot.

People are going to start looking down from office windows any minute.

I take my rainbow scarf off and tie it on my head. I pull it close around my face. Nobody would ever guess who is hiding under it. And just in time, too.

With a singing growl, Mama mushes through a line or two:

"I got a gal, she's six feet tall,
Sleeps in the kitchen with her feet in the hall."

On the last line, she stomps the ground. A little public dancing! Just to pep things up. I glance around. Nobody is looking, yet. Thank goodness!

I catch up with her and begin to chatter. With a sweet smile, she gives me her full attention. She gives the scarf around my head some attention, too, but says nothing about it. We may make it to the car with no more singing or dancing if I'm lucky.

We two are close already but very different. This is why she can read my mind . . . and still not read all of it.

She says I am not interested in Troy?

Troy could be my light at the end of the tunnel, this long tunnel I am crawling through. From one mother to two mothers. From an only child to a girl who has a sister. From Dad's best pal to one of his two pals. From proper-perfect to . . . what? To a new me?

This new me is not interested in this new guy?

I'm interested.

I can't wait to tell Elaine.

CHAPTER TWO
Elaine

"So tell me! Come on, Elaine, open up," Nita says.

My best friend wants to hear about my twin. I have been talking to Nita about Emily ever since I got back from Florida a couple of months ago. Now my twin is here in Corte Madera. She and Mama are driving home from a day in San Francisco right now. Nita is about to die of curiosity. She can't believe she is going to meet a total stranger who looks just like me.

I decide to torture her.

"How do you like our new beds? How about the spreads? Do you like the color?" I ask, smoothing the spread with one hand and gazing down at it.

For a second she looks at the bright yellow spreads. Her eyes follow my hand. Then she scowls and looks up at me. She gives her head one shake, fanning her short, black hair straight out so that it smacks against her cheeks.

"If you don't tell me about Emily . . . see

these claws of mine?" She holds out her fingers. Her fingernails are short and stubby. "I'll rip this spread apart." She claws the air. "It's not enough that I was gone when she got here. The shopping in L.A. is great, by the way. When you called about Emily, I rushed home last night and ran over here this morning and the Southern Princess is out." She makes a growling noise in her throat.

"Calm down," I say in a maddening, mother tone. "I am going to tell you about Emily, okay? But first things first." I get up and go to the dresser. I pick up a photograph and hand it to her.

"My new guy," I say, "the one I met in Florida." I jump on the bed behind her and look over her shoulder. We study the photo of my blond boyfriend's face. I breathe deeply and whisper, "I think I really like him. His name is Dean."

Nita looks at Dean's photo. "I can't argue with this," she says, waving the photo. "He makes me hyperventilate. I want to hear all about him." Carefully, she puts the photo on the bed, face down. "But"—she slows her voice—"the first thing I want to hear about is still Emily."

"Okay, okay." I sit back and she turns toward me. Torture time is over. But what's to tell? "You already know the really exciting stuff. Like how my parents were divorced and my father got custody of Emily and me. We couldn't speak for ourselves, you see. The only

reason he got away with it was because he was
a big lawyer in a little town and Mama was
nobody. I mean by local standards. She lived in
the Mexican migrant community. The barrio.
I'm talking *poor*. Here she was, an up and coming young social worker from across the tracks
when she married my father. Emily and I were
born and then . . . soon there was the divorce.
She wanted to stay home and take care of us.
This is when she moved back to the barrio and
stayed in her mother's little house. By the way,
that was an okay little house. It just couldn't
compete with my father's house. The guy lives
in the biggest house in town. An updated
Southern mansion. He's got tennis courts, a
great big pool, and jacuzzis all over the place."
I fall back and throw out my arms as though
overcome.

Nita gives the bed an impatient jiggle.

"Don't tell me what I already know. I already know how your mother couldn't stand being separated from you guys. You've already
told me how she tried to kidnap you and Emily,
and how she got away with only you. Worse
luck!"

I rise up and punch Nita on the shoulder.

She sways with the punch and, without missing a beat, she says, "So how about it? Do you
think you can tell me about the Southern Princess? What is she like?"

The Southern Princess. That is what I used
to call Emily.

* * *

Before Mama and I went to Florida to see my twin, I thought about Emily a lot. I didn't think I would like her. I dreaded meeting this rich girl that my mother talked about incessantly. "My Emily, my Emily!" she would say. Was I jealous? I didn't think so at the time.

I knew Emily grew up with things I could never have, but the most important thing in the world . . . she didn't have that and I did. Our mother. So, if I wasn't jealous, why didn't I like this sister I had never really known? That's a hard one.

I got a little piece of the answer when we got to Fern, Florida.

I absolutely hated my father, sight unseen. I sneaked away from the barrio where Mama and I were hiding out and went straight to my father's office. He is a judge now. He has a whole suite of offices with sky-high windows and thick carpets. I had to pretend I was my sister, the twin he raised, because Mama didn't want him to know we were in town. She was afraid he would charge her with kidnapping me. After all these years, she was still afraid!

Not me. I had to see the guy. I meant to tell him how much I hated him. I hadn't been with him for more than five minutes when I knew I couldn't do that. Looking into his pink, wrinkled face I could see my own blue eyes. And most of all, I could see my temper flash across his face when, acting as his other daughter, I sassed him. We both got red in the face and began to sweat and . . . I knew I was home.

Later, after Mama confronted him, I told him
how I felt about what he did to Mama and me.
And Emily. He is sorry. He is trying to make
it up to us. Emily and I are going to visit back
and forth from Florida to California as often as
we can.

I love my twin. But I know now that I was
jealous of her. The reason was because she had
our father all to herself all those years.

She still acts as though she owns him. But I
am his daughter, too, and Emily will have to
face up to it.

To Nita I say, "Don't call Emily that. I know,
I know, I started that Southern Princess thing,
but she's not like that. I don't want her to hear
us call her that. She . . ." I stop. I hear a car.

Nita and I both run to the window and watch
Mama and Emily get out of the car and come
up the walk. It is still a shock, watching Emily.
It is like looking in a mirror.

"Why . . . it's you! She looks just like you. I'll
never be able to tell you women apart." Nita
wrings her hands and jumps back from the
window. She is tiny like my mother and can
jump around in a small room without bumping
into the furniture.

I hear Emily running toward our bedroom.
She starts yelling "Elaine" before she gets to
the door. She stops when she sees Nita.

I look at my sister.

I will never get used to it . . . my face on
somebody else. My tall body, my long red hair.

I have to tell myself, that is not me. That is another. My other.

Being separated all our lives, Emily and I didn't grow up wearing the same clothes, but we might as well have. We wear the same look. Creative. Not junky but easy. And lots of color. We both mix colors that the kids around here won't mix. Like Russia-on-a-winter-night colors . . . we mix those with the hottest, sweatiest, sexiest colors we can scrounge. If there is a difference in how Emily and I dress, it is like this: while she is layering on more of those cold, winter-night clouds, I am pulling on more of the South Seas' sunsets. When we finish dressing we are like the upside-down twins. Her tops may match my bottoms or vice versa.

Today, her T-shirt is a mauve thing that hugs her breasts. My tee is a loose sunburst tie-dye. She's wearing bibs, and her mustard-colored pants are hitched up by silver and black suspenders. Pretty good, but look at me. Under my sunburst tie-dye, I've got on streaked maroon and chocolate pants. Over all of it I'm wearing a black vest with big, gold metal buttons. How do I do it? It takes time and talent. With just a nudge, Emily could cross over from her almost-there to my perfect.

Of course, she'd have to get rid of that rainbow scarf. There's nothing wrong with the scarf itself, but I could get sick of looking at it. Doesn't she ever take it off?

* * *

My almost-there twin is almost in the room but not quite. Why doesn't she come in?

Emily looks at Nita and hesitates. If there is a real difference between us it is my twin's shyness. I jump up, grab her by the arm, and pull her into the room.

"This is my best friend, Nita," I say. As soon as the words are out of my mouth I realize that this is no longer quite true. Is Emily my best friend now? I'll have to figure that out later. "This is Emily," I tell Nita.

The twin beds aren't wide enough for all three of us to sit on and face each other, so we get on the floor. I have this fluffy rug, a black and green one that Mama hates because loose fibers stick to my bottom when I get up. I jump up and slap my backside to knock the fibers off.

"Be back in a minute," I say. I can't get into a deep-down, earthy woman conversation without something to drink.

I find my mother in the kitchen unloading groceries. I kiss the top of her head and help her, chattering all the while.

"How'd it go?" I ask. "What did Emily think of your class? Did the guys put on a good show for her?" I like my mother's drama class. Some of those kids are so talented! But Mama won't let me go very often. Outsiders aren't allowed every day.

Mama puts a bag of noodles on the counter. She turns her dark eyes upon me. Why can't I do that? Look gorgeous and serious at the same time?

"I want to talk to you, Elaine. We may have a problem. No, I don't want to talk now. Later, when Emily is taking a bath." She puts a huge tomato on the counter. Then a green pepper, an onion, a whole garlic bulb, a zucchini, and a handful of fresh basil. My stomach contracts. I am so decadent! I get hungry at the sight of luscious veggies.

"You got it," I say. I grab three bottles of seltzer out of the refrigerator and open them. They start spewing foam. The bubbles tickles my nose. I am twitching my nose like a rabbit when I get back to the bedroom. Emily and Nita look up at me.

Dramatically, I hold the three bottles over their heads. Then, with a flourish, I sit down. The way I do it, it is an art. I slide one leg under me, bend one knee, and ease down like the dancer I am. Perfect!

I have a great body and I like it when people tell me about it. I am handing out the fizzing bottles when I notice a strange silence. Nita and my twin aren't talking.

"Did you see how I got to the floor?" I ask loudly. "I'll bet you guys can't sit down from a standing position like that. While carrying three open bottles. And not spill any."

More silence.

Nita chugalugs and puts her bottle down. "Got to go," she says.

I can't believe this. She has been waiting for days to meet my twin. Now she has to go?

I argue and yell but I don't change her mind.

When Nita is below my bedroom window she gives me a short wave and disappears around the corner.

"What got into her?" I ask, looking at my twin. Emily drinks her soda. She takes the bottle from her mouth and cuts her blue eyes up at me. A challenging squint. I know that look. It's mine.

"You know why she left, don't you?" I say.

"It's not important," she says.

"What!" Is she kidding? Nita is one of my two best friends.

Emily sets her drink on the floor, just beyond the rug. "I don't want to talk about her. I've got something to tell you." Her eyes go wide. She swings her hair back. She smiles. She doesn't smile. She smiles again. This woman is excited, I tell myself. I'll have to dig it out of her about Nita when she calms down.

"Tell," I say.

"Elaine, I'm getting some strong signals about a guy."

"I already know that. How long have you been dating Kyle? That's ancient history, Emily. Tell me something new," I say.

She waves her hand as though she is pushing something away.

"No, no," she says. "This isn't about Kyle. Elaine, this is about someone else. If I tell you, you won't tell Mama, will you? I don't think she is ready for this."

She is bending forward and I lean away from her. Cautiously, I say, "I won't tell. But who is it? You didn't seem impressed by any of the guys you've met so far." I am thinking fast. She's been here less than a week. She has met the kids I hang out with. She's been playing tennis with a couple of the guys, but I didn't notice any hormone attacks when she was with them. And I think I would. Emily and I can see things about each other. It is like we can read what goes on inside. We call it our twin-sense.

The other day, I asked my biology teacher about it. I asked how Emily and I can feel so much alike on the inside. After all, we have been separated all our lives. She told me that what Emily and I have is not simple ESP. It is a built-in kind of chemistry that gives us our twin-sense.

But now . . . I am stumped.

Emily's eyes positively glisten. She leans closer to me.

"It's Troy."

I must look funny because she says, "Elaine, don't be like that."

Slowly, I say, "Troy."

Troy is good looking. Sweet. A real pal. But I saw Troy when he arrived at Juvenile Hall. He was one broken kid. As my mother says, what Troy needs is a safe environment. For months, maybe years. Is my twin a safe environment?

"You think you're interested in Troy?" I ask, not sure I heard right.

"Admit it. You know he's gorgeous. Sexy. Adorable. What more could anyone want?"

"How about most people could want to know each other better? I mean you just met him. You two, you don't know each other. And, anyway, how did you guys find time to talk? Mama keeps those drama class kids busy. I'm surprised you got to say two words to him."

"He made the time." She says this proudly. "He came over to me and we talked. At first he thought I was you. But I told him who I was. After that, we sort of got close. It happened so fast! In five minutes, I knew something was going on between us."

"I can see that something was going on. But maybe just for you. What makes you think that Troy . . . that he felt the same way?" I mean, this could be something Emily wants, not necessarily something that really happened. I know. I could build a good case if we were talking about me instead of her. I hate to admit it, but I believe what I want to believe sometimes. Maybe she does, too.

"Because he said so," she snaps back at me. She doesn't like my question. In a minute, she adds, "Not in so many words. What he said was he wants me to come back tomorrow. He can't wait."

"In that case . . ." I begin. Hey, it really does look like something is going on here. I mean, if he said so, that changes things, doesn't it? I start to feel Emily's excitement.

I look at my twin's glowing face. Am I ever going to look that beautiful? I know, I know, feature for feature we look identical, but right now her face . . . it is one big glow. Anything that makes her look like that . . . can it be all bad?

My doubts are melting away. Maybe Emily would be good for Troy and vice versa. They are both a little bit goofy. Maybe this thing between them, maybe it is okay. I feel like the room is filling up with golden lights.

I grab Emily by the hand. "How are you going to see him?"

"He wants me to come back to class tomorrow. Do you think Mama will let me? I've got to go! You've got to help me convince her that I should go. Maybe I'll get interested in drama. Something like that. Do you think that will work with Mama?"

We are holding hands. We are all smiles. Mama comes to the door.

"I need some help in the kitchen. Whose turn is it?"

I know she knows. It's my turn.

My twin cooked the whole supper last night. Some Southern food. Fried okra, et cetera. It wasn't too awful.

"While you two slave away over supper, I'll get my bath. Don't hurry me, my slaves." Emily heads for the bathroom, dragging a Japanese kimona after her.

In the kitchen, my mother turns to me. She takes the chopping knife out of my hand.

"Elaine, we have something to talk about. Your sister. She's light-headed over a boy at the school. Do you remember Troy?"

So she knows.

"Yeah?" I say, trying to look surprised. "You think Emily likes Troy?"

"I have her in my care for one week and what happens? She gets interested in this sweet, troubled boy. I don't think he is quite that interested in her, but Troy loves attention. He probably will respond if she persists. What is to be done? I don't want him upset. And I certainly don't want my daughter to look foolish, to make a grab for the first boy who needs her attention. What goes on with Emily? Does a dependent type like Troy make her feel strong? Is that it?" She looks at me but she is not seeing me; she is seeing Emily. "You know what I think?" she continues, "I think she is temporarily off balance, because of all this change. Leaving home. Being here with us in a strange place. She has always been so sheltered. I must remember that. I think she'll come to her senses in a day or two. Don't you?"

"Maybe but, oh, oh!" I have had a ghastly thought. "What would Dad say if he knew?" I can see his angry face. One of the judge's daughters involved with a first offender? I get the hiccups when I think of my father's reaction. When I picture Emily telling him about her new boyfriend, the hiccups accelerate.

"I am not going to worry about that. It will be his problem," Mama says.

I can see that I have struck a nerve. With sudden urgency, she adds, "Elaine, you must help. Stay close to your sister. Take her to your dance class. Give her a party. Make her know how much you want her here. Maybe this is all she needs. Maybe if we can fill up her time she won't look around for some foolish attachment."

What my mother says makes sense.

What Dad will think has to be considered, too. Not because he is always right. He isn't. But because I want my father to like me.

Emily has always been Dad's one and only child. They were as close as a parent and a child can get. I grew up far away from our father so I never knew this kind of father-daughter closeness. Now, I have a chance to make Dad love me that way, too.

I am going to visit Emily and Dad during the Christmas holidays. Dad was insistent that I come. I know he wants to get to know me, but if he finds out I encouraged Emily's interest in a guy who got in trouble with the law, I could lose my chance with him.

I think about it.

At last, my twin-sense turns on. And I know ... if I don't stand by Emily ... it will be like trashing myself. It's no contest when it comes to my twin.

Sorry Dad. Sorry Mama. If Emily needs me, I've got to help her.

CHAPTER THREE
Emily

I come out of the bathroom in my Japanese kimono. Elaine is waiting for me. She watches as I tie my sash.

"What do you want me to do, Emily?" she asks. She is sitting on her bed. I sit opposite her on mine.

"I want Troy's phone number. I want to call him," I say.

"You want the Juvenile Hall number? You're not supposed to call there," she says, but her blue eyes light up.

"Please, Elaine. Do you know the number?"

"Be right back." She goes out and returns with my mother's school folder. She opens it, flips through it, stops on a page, and hands it to me.

I stretch to the bedside telephone.

"Go!" she says, and I dial.

"May I speak to Troy Chavez . . ." I begin. Elaine snatches the telephone out of my hand.

In a precise voice, she says, "Please bring the Chavez boy to the telephone. Tell him his aunt wishes to speak to him." She looks nervous. I feel hiccups coming on. All at once, Elaine relaxes.

"Hi, Troy. Here's somebody that wants to talk to you." She hands the phone to me.

I say "Hello." I tell him my name. I can picture the surprise on his face. I get nervous and look up at Elaine. She raises a fist.

"Emily?" He sounds puzzled. "We had better make this quick. What do you want?"

"I am coming back to drama class tomorrow," I remind him. Still nothing on the other end of the line. Elaine says I am shy, but this guy is state of the art. "Do you think we could talk some more?" I ask. Is this me talking? I have always waited for the guy to make the plans. But I am doing it, aren't I? Surprise!

"You are?" he says.

"I want to see you again, Troy." I say. My twin puts both hands over her mouth in mock shock.

He hesitates. After a second, he blurts, "Hey, that's radical! You want to see me?"

"I felt something good going on between us. I felt like we are going to be friends. Good friends. Maybe more." I have softened my voice and talk more slowly.

"You felt that way? About me?"

How can a great-looking guy like Troy be surprised that a girl likes him?

"I like you," I tell him. "Do you want me to come tomorrow?"

"Try me!" he says excitedly. "Just try me!"

I whisper "Good-bye" and hang up. I cut my eyes over at my twin.

"I can't believe you," she says, wide-eyed. "I thought I was the bold one." She is smiling, but a serious look crosses her face. "Don't take this wrong, but aren't you moving a little fast?"

I slink down and stretch out. I ooze around on the bed like a cat.

"You're just jealous," I say.

Elaine laughs, but then she thinks about it. "You may be right. My Dean is so far away! I wish he hadn't gone to college in New England. I wish he had come out here to a California college instead," she says wistfully.

"Let's talk about Troy." It is not a request. It is a command. "I want you to tell me everything you know. From start to finish. Nita lived a couple of doors down from Troy, didn't she?" I know this because Nita told me so this afternoon when Elaine left us alone. As soon as I mentioned the guy's name, Nita began her weird story. I quit talking to her when she said Troy stole a car. How ridiculous! I don't see what Elaine sees in this girl, Nita.

I glance at my twin, but she isn't looking at me. She falls back on her bed and laces her fingers over her chest. She is studying the ceiling. I think she is trying to replay all she knows about Troy. I get ready to listen.

I fall back on my bed. Without thinking, I lace my fingers across my chest. Then I notice what I have done. I didn't exactly copy my twin—I probably would have flopped back in this position if I had been alone. I am learning that twins are strange people. Our bodies move in similar ways. Sometimes without our instructions!

"Troy moved from Oakland to San Francisco a few months ago." My sister begins. "Nita said that Troy's parents were strange from the start. Everybody else on the block went to work each day, but not them. Troy was late for school a lot. He said he had to fix breakfast for the family before he could leave."

"Not that part. I don't want to know about his family. Tell me about him. Did he have a girl?" We have turned sideways and are looking at each other.

"A girl? I don't know. But Nita says she never saw him out anywhere. According to her Troy was always at home. Always doing chores. That's funny, because how much is there to do when he is the only kid in the family? The whole family is in custody now, of course." She says this so casually it takes me a second to get it. In custody? Does that mean in jail? Elaine isn't looking at me so she doesn't see my mouth hanging open. After a pause, she goes on. "His mother is in rehabilitation and his father went to prison a couple of months ago. Oh, you didn't know that? Yeah. Something to do with drugs."

This isn't what I had expected to hear. I am relieved when Elaine says she has told me all she knows. I switch the subject to Dean, a subject my twin enjoys.

* * *

The next morning, when I hear my mother get up I jump out of bed. I pull on pants and a shirt. The shirt is an expensive one my stepmother bought me. It is pinky-purple. She says it is my color. I button the shirt and hurry into the kitchen. The smell of cinnamon toast is all over the place. Mama is getting up from the table.

"Where are you going?" she asks me. She raises her cup. She puts it in the dishwasher. She does everything in split seconds.

I laugh merrily. "With you, of course," I say.

She stops and puts her hands on the sink and drums it like she's playing a piano.

"Not two days in a row, Emily. It is not a good idea." Her black eyes move over my face. "I thought you were upset by the way the kids express themselves in their dramas. They get down to it, don't they? You see, that's part of the cure, so to speak. These kids, Maya and Troy and the rest, haven't had many opportunities to act out their emotions in a safe place. That's why they are excitable. It is exciting for them to be able to do this without fear of . . . without fear. I am glad you are interested in my kids, but today? No."

She pecks me on the cheek and hurries past me. I can hear her go out of the door and start the car.

I trudge back into the bedroom and wake up my twin.

"You've got to help me, Elaine," I say, shaking her shoulder. She opens her eyes, mumbling. Then she sits straight up. "She didn't take you with her?"

I shake my head. I sit on the edge of her bed. "Elaine, I told Troy I'd come back today. I want to go."

"If Mama said you can't go . . ." She peers into my face. "But she didn't say we couldn't go into town, town being San Francisco. Come on, we'll go into town and work something out from there."

"Like what?" I ask.

"I don't know yet," she says impatiently.

It helps that she is on my side. So why do I feel like crying? It's too much. Everything. Even Troy. It is hard to admit it but . . . he didn't sound so glad to hear from me last night. Not at first. I had to push to get him interested, and I don't know why I did that.

I am last out of the house. Elaine drags me behind her, pulling on my arm.

"Hurry, we're going to miss the bus," she says. "Oh, for Pete's sake, there it goes." She sits down on the curb. I stumble down beside her.

It is too much. I start to cry.

"You aren't crying!" She jumps up as though scandalized.

I blubber. "I just wish I were back home," I say. The thought hasn't entered my head until this minute.

My twin sits down and puts an arm around me.

"Emily"—Elaine's voice turns down, low and soft—"I'd miss you so bad I'd die. I'll do anything to make you like it here."

I lean against her and rub my wet face on her hair.

"I've got an idea," she says like she's talking to an idiot child. "How would you like to shop while we wait for the next bus?"

There is a row of shops right behind us. The windows are draped with have-to-have clothes, and I am loaded with spending money—the kind Elaine calls play-dough. Dad handed me this play-dough a couple of weeks ago. For the trip, he said. Go have fun, he said. He has never given me this much before. And this was twice as much for him to give because he sent Elaine the same amount. I didn't know whether to be grateful or disgusted at his oh-so-sudden generosity. It was plain to see he got carried away at the idea of having two daughters instead of one. Instead of just me.

Elaine pulls me up from the curb and we go in and out of a couple of shops. I like everything I see. I am trailing my hand down one shirt after another, but Elaine tugs me away.

"We've got to get you out of those sickly pinks, purples, and lavenders," she says. "Also that rainbow rag." She points disgustedly at the scarf around my neck.

"You don't like my clothes?" I am surprised.

"I like your clothes. But you can do better.

Besides, you told me your stepmother picks them out for you."

I straighten up. She straightens up. We are tall. With a sweep of both hands, she swings her long, red hair from her neck to her back. I am doing the same thing at the same time.

These are my moves! These are the things I do!

We both look angry. Then we start to laugh.

"This twin business . . . it's going to take some getting used to," she says. We start toward the next shop. I grab her by the sleeve.

"Just for the record, I didn't say my stepmother picked out my clothes. I said she helped me. I make the final decision." Most of the time.

She has found a shirt and is holding it up to my shoulders.

"No. Not right." She puts it back on the rack.

I pull out a vest. I don't know why I like it. I never wear this color. My stepmother says it doesn't look good on redheads. It is wine red. Like spilled vinegar, the deep red kind called balsamic. I hold the vest against me and look in a mirror.

"That's it!" Elaine has whirled around and is pushing the vest against my shoulders. "You did it. All by yourself. Now I know you're in love."

I look at her questioningly.

"Love gives us courage," she intones.

I wear my new vest out of the store. Elaine walks me into a juice bar. We both order kiwi sorbet. Elaine's head comes close to mine. "Now we'll make some plans," she says. "When we get to San Francisco, we'll drop by the school and tell Mama we came to town to shop. She'll buy that."

"But . . . I've got to talk to Troy. Alone," I insist. I must find out if I really like the guy. And how much.

"You will. We'll drop by the school during lunch break." She wrinkles her brow. "I wish I had worn some of your clothes this morning." Suddenly, a light bulb seems to flash on in her face. She grabs a corner of my rainbow scarf. She unties it and pulls it off. In a second, she has it around her neck.

"What are you doing?" I ask. "I thought you hated that scarf." I haven't told her my scarf is like a good luck charm. Dad has had it ever since I can remember. When I was leaving, he tied it around my neck and said, "This scarf . . . it will bring you love." I don't know what he had in mind, but I think it's going to work for me.

"I hated it an hour ago. Now I love it." She ties the ends and lets them hang off one shoulder. She finishes with a flourish and looks at me with a big smile. "Who am I?"

"What do you mean?" I ask.

"If you were Mama and you saw me coming through the classroom door wearing this scarf . . . who would you think I am?" she asks, still smiling big.

"Oh!" I begin, "so you are me. You go in the classroom. You get to see Troy and I don't!"

She holds up a finger.

"I go in and wave at Mama from the back of the room. In my best Southern accent, I say I just dropped in a minute to let her know that Elaine (that's you) and I are shopping. I say you are still uptown looking at clothes. Then I walk around a minute," she says.

"That's it?" I ask.

"Of course not, silly. I show Mama that I (you) am not interested in Troy. I talk to Maya. I talk to Ellie. I talk to a couple of the guys. But I ignore Troy. Now, you could never do that, could you? Then, very casually, I drop a note on Troy's desk. It will tell him I am Elaine. It will tell him that Emily is waiting for him in the parking lot. Lunch break comes. He goes out. I stay inside with Mama. Troy finds you. You can cover him with kisses and nobody will ever know. Like it?"

It's complicated. Too complicated, it seems to me, but I don't argue.

"Do you think it will work?" I can barely breathe I am so excited. I wish I were as brave as my twin. She knows I wouldn't have the nerve to do what she is going to do.

"It's done," she says. "By the way, how did you like my Southern accent?"

She sounds a lot more deep South than I do. The test is this: will our mother be able to tell the difference?

"Stop worrying," she says, reading my mind.

* * *

The bus stops. We get off and wander down toward the bay to wait for the lunch hour.

"Are you calming down?" she wants to know.

"Yes," I say. But I'm not.

We are in a little park. Elaine sits on the grass and pats a space beside her. I crumple down and am getting comfortable when she says, "I know. We'll talk about Dad. That's a soothing subject."

This makes me want to scream. We have already had talks about Dad. How much more is there to say?

In a small voice she says, "It must have been wonderful growing up with him. In the same house. Having breakfast with your own father every morning!" She looks at me, starry-eyed. "Did he carry you upstairs every night and put you to bed? Did he tell you bedtime stories?"

"He was a good dad," I say wearily. It is true. But I have told Elaine everything I can think of about Life with Father. From the year one. Now she wants me to start all over. I hold my wrist up to my face and look at my watch. "Hey, by the time we walk to the school it will be lunchtime. Let's go."

I walk fast and Elaine follows me silently. In ten minutes we reach the school. My sister gives me a parting look and goes inside.

I find the parking lot and stand behind a bus.

I wait. I look at my watch. Did something go wrong?

I hear footsteps.

"Emily!"

I turn around. It is Troy. He runs toward me. "You came," he says. He looks glad to see me. His dark eyes shine. Our smiles go all over our faces.

"Yeah," I say.

"I'm glad," he says.

"Me too," I say. I see him look at my new vest and I hope I look good, but I can't think of anything else to say. Troy puts his hands in his pockets and steps back. This is awkward.

"Did Elaine . . . did she do all right?" I ask, stumbling over my words like a little kid.

"I'm here. Whatever she did, it worked." After another silence, Troy says, "At first I thought she was you. You know, the accent. Then she put this note on my desk." He pulls a piece of paper out of his pocket.

I look at the note. You'd think it was the Declaration of Independence, the way we study that note. Why can't I think of anything to say? Why can't we get easy with each other? Time is slipping by. Soon he will have to go back inside. The way this is going . . . my father could be here with us—and approve!

Now I step back. I am getting embarrassed.

Troy starts talking about a soccer game. I am not interested in soccer. What a bore! Maybe I am not interested in this guy after all.

Maybe the feeling that I had for him yesterday, maybe that was just an emotional glitch in the machinery of my heart. Mama will be glad to hear I have recovered.

Mama. I get a warm glow just thinking of her. And then I get worried. I wasn't comfortable with the idea that I might cause her concern by coming here today. I think about how easy she made it for me to fit into her family of two, she and Elaine. She has enough affection for both of us with some left over.

My father is also affectionate. He, too, tried to make room for both Elaine and me. I am sure he did a good job.

Every time I tell myself a lie, half of my brain goes to sleep. It just shuts down. The only way I can turn it back on is to start over. With the truth.

No, my dad didn't do a good job. I am sure he tried. But he let me down. Last summer when my twin came into our lives, I found myself shoved almost out of the picture.

This hurt. It still hurts even now, just remembering it. I love my twin, but I can't help but wish I still came first with my father.

Grow up! I tell myself. A grown woman, which I am, doesn't go on needing her father forever. A grown woman finds a man of her own.

I look at Troy. He has stopped talking and is studying me. He holds up the note. "It says here you want to talk to me."

He shoves his dark hair back from his face with a quick jab of his hand. Like me, he has turned nervous. For some reason, this calms me down. I know I can put him at ease and this makes me feel strong.

I reach out. My fingers find his hand. At once, he smiles. The warmest, biggest smile! I can tell he likes me.

"I missed you. I couldn't wait to get here." The minute the words come out of my mouth I know they are true. What has been the matter with me? This guy, he is gorgeous! Creamy skin, black eyes. Let's mention his body. He is not tall for a guy, about my height, but he has a perfect body. Nice shoulders. No butt at all. How do guys like this sit down? How do they make it through the day without being ravished by every girl they meet? Love him? I'd have to be crazy not to.

When I take his hand in mine I get warm all the way up to my neck.

"I dreamed about you last night, Troy. Can you guess what I dreamed?" I lean toward this good-looking guy and put my other hand on his arm.

"What?" he asks. His face gets a caved-in look. His lips part. His eyes are fastened on mine.

"That you kissed me," I say softly.

Troy comes closer. He lifts my arms and puts them around his neck. "I don't know about dreams. They don't have much to do with real life. But that one, that's one dream we can make come true." He lowers his face.

I notice his nose. It is round on the end, not pointed like Kyle's. He is so close his nose touches my cheek.

Then Troy kisses me. His lips cover mine

very gently and my hands slip up his neck. I'm not counting seconds, but this kiss doesn't want to stop. I turn my face just a little bit. My mouth rubs across his. I turn my face the other way. The skin on our lips turns hot. I want some more. But Troy draws back.

His breath is coming fast. He blinks at me.

"Do you like me, Troy? If you do, please tell me," I whisper. I ache to hear it.

His hands fall from my waist and he says, "I had no idea you liked me so much."

That's not what I wanted to hear.

"My secret is out." I don't mean to sound sarcastic, but it happens. He looks puzzled. "Of course I like you," I say. "That's why I'm here. Now, tell me. How do you feel about me?"

Troy steps back and shoves his hands in his pockets. I can see his fingers wiggling nervously through the cloth of his pants.

"I don't know, Emily. It would be awfully easy to like a girl like you. You are pretty and sexy and all that. But the main thing is . . . you are nice to me." He pauses. His thick, dark eyebrows draw into a small scowl. "You are *too* nice to me and that is what I don't understand. Where are you coming from?"

I don't like the turn this conversation has taken. I look around. I spread out my hands.

In a stronger voice Troy says, "You. The social worker's daughter. Why should you like a guy like me?"

I scowl, too. "What's so terrible about being a first offender?"

He gives me a funny look and shakes his head.

"You don't know anything about it, do you?"

"About what?" I ask, feeling stupid.

"About growing up in Oakland in a housing project. About having parents who are dealing. I'm talking guns and dead kids. At my front door." With a look of impatience, he turns his back on me.

For a minute I don't know what to do. I have never known a guy in Troy's situation. Not up close.

Take Kyle. A boy born with a silver spoon in his mouth. There was never a moment and there never will be when I can feel sorry for Kyle. He doesn't need anybody's sympathy or anybody's encouragement. Kyle is a nice guy with a nice future. With an affluent college professor Dad behind him. And, although I never thought about it before, now I see it as an enormous plus that Kyle is on the safe side of the law. Mama can say first offenders are just like the rest of us. I may agree. But anyway you look at it, a first offender is in a shaky position.

My father will never understand how I could fall for a guy like Troy. But I am not my father.

No matter what anyone says about it one thing is certain. The way I feel about Troy is nobody's business but mine.

I look at Troy's back. I feel a tug at my heart. Sure, I had romantic ideas about him and I still do. But right now I am talking to a guy whose head is hanging. He is talking about himself like he is a throwaway.

I run to him. I hold him. I have to say it.

"You were right, Troy, when you said I like you a lot . . . because I do."

He holds me away from him. For a minute, I think he is angry.

"You don't mean that!" His voice shakes. With hope . . . not anger.

My heart is doing somersaults.

"I do. I really do," I say.

With a sudden movement, he pulls me to him. Not to kiss. He holds me so tightly I can't breathe.

I get one of those absolute, has-to-be-right realizations. I came here today to make something happen. But that changed. Instead of me making something happen, something is really happening.

To Troy and me.

I don't care what this guy has done before.

He is my guy, now.

CHAPTER FOUR
Elaine

"Elaine, will you please come here."

My mother's voice is too polite. She gets polite in a chilly way when she's mad at me.

"What is it, Mama?" I sit down across the kitchen table from her. She pours a cup of espresso. It tastes like cough syrup to me, which she knows, so she doesn't offer me any.

"I want you to start from the beginning and tell me what was going on at school today." She holds the cup in both hands but doesn't sip. Her black eyes are enormous.

I can't lie to those black eyes.

Once I got past the excitement this morning of pretending I was my sister, I got this awful let-down feeling. I kept remembering my mother's face when I told her that "Elaine" was uptown shopping. I kept touching Emily's scarf. I smoothed it around my neck and fiddled with the ends that flowed over my shoulder. With my fingers I was saying, look Ma, I've got to be Emily. See, I am wearing her scarf. You believe me, don't you?

My mother had glanced up at me, started to look down, then jerked her head back up and stared. That's when I turned around, dropped Emily's note on Troy's desk, and hurried out. I waited for my twin at the bus stop. It seemed like an hour. I missed two buses before she came. When she finally arrived, she looked all aglow and trembly.

Some of the excitement came back for me as I listened to her talk about Troy, but by the time we got home I felt lousy.

"What's the matter with you?" Emily wanted to know.

"Maybe we shouldn't have done this. I know, I know. I planned the whole thing. But I hate lying to Mama."

Now, I look into my mother's eyes, my mouth comes open, and I stammer. "What do you mean? I don't know ... what you're talking about."

Emily comes in and stands beside the table between Mama and me. She is just out of the bathtub. As usual, she took an hour, lying in the tub like a dead porpoise under her seafoam bubbles. The Southern Princess doesn't know the meaning of the word *share.* At her home in Florida, she has a whole jacuzzi to herself. There are five bathrooms in that big house and only three people. Why should she hurry? But here we have only one small bathroom and no jacuzzi. We form a line at the door.

I hold my nose. Bubble bath "perfume"

stinks up the whole room. Why does Emily like that sickening smell? Oil of eucalyptus. Barf!

"I have something to say," she says in a small voice.

I glance at Mama. Very slowly, she puts her cup down.

Emily puts a hand on Mama's arm.

"I feel rotten about what I did," she says, "but I had to see Troy."

Mama cocks her head to one side. She waits and Emily says it again. "I had to see Troy. I wanted to tell you this morning but I couldn't get started. I . . . I guess I like him a lot, Mama."

Mama puts her hand over Emily's.

"If you had told me, I might have been able to arrange something with Troy's counselor. Bring the boy here, maybe. Have a cookout in the backyard. Or go to the beach." She draws back a little. "You didn't have to plan some elaborate charade just to get to see him. That's the kind of thing Elaine likes to organize. But you . . . I didn't think you . . ."

Suddenly, they both look at me.

"Don't look at me," I say in a loud voice. "I'm not the one that had to have a great romance."

They keep looking at me.

I sigh. "Okay, it was my idea, what you call the charade. But I don't see why . . ." I am about to say that I can't see why I have to take all the blame for the activity of Emily's hormones. I get interrupted.

"She was just trying to help me. The whole

thing was my fault, Mama. Can you forgive me?" Emily says.

"If you won't do this again. By that I mean ... you girls may fool other people with your look-alike faces as long as you don't do any harm. But not me. Never again. Do I make myself clear?" She stops and takes a sip of espresso. "Emily goes back to Florida day after tomorrow. How do you want to spend your last day here, Emily? Or do I need to ask?"

"Can you bring Troy home with you tomorrow night, Mama?" Emily asks. Like me, she has a wide mouth. When we smile, we show teeth, gums, and tonsils. She's doing it now. "Can we all go to the beach?"

I have been dreaming of a day at the beach with Dean. But he is far away. He would be so sorry if he knew what he is missing. I have this new bathing suit. In it, I look like Miss-America-get-a-shape. I was saving my suit for this dream I have: Dean and me on a Florida beach. That dream can't come true, so I guess I'll wear it tomorrow.

Morning finds Emily and me shopping for goodies. We get home from the supermarket with a big pineapple to put in the picnic hamper. Around the pineapple, we stack lots of grapes and cheese, fresh-baked San Francisco bread, and a thermos of herb tea. We leave a little space for Mama's specialty, chimichangas, wrapped in foil to keep them hot.

I juice a bunch of carrots and papayas together and we are ready by the time Mama and Troy arrive. The sun is setting when we leave the house.

It is one of those twilights when the beach turns silvery pink and the water is the color of mercury. A big moon waits, very pale, for night to come. I gather wood for a fire. Emily takes Troy by the hand and leads him off. Soon, their two figures are tiny blurs that follow the edge of the surf.

"What do you think?" I ask Mama. We are sitting by the fire, taking pineapple slices in our teeth to keep the juice from running down our chins.

"I like it. They're having a good time. Emily leaves tomorrow. They'll have sweet memories—and probably forget about each other. Right?"

"Right," I agree.

The sweethearts return and we eat our supper listening to bird cries and the drumbeat of waves. We take our time. Finally we pack up.

We have to drive into San Francisco to take Troy back to Juvenile Hall before we can go home.

When we get to the hall, Emily insists on going inside, at least as far as the waiting room. She wants to see how Troy lives, she tells him.

"Aw, Emily, a college dormitory it is not," he says.

"It's all the same to me. It's where you live," she says.

She marches ahead beside Mama. Troy hangs back.

"It won't kill her," I tell him. "She's tougher than she looks. Besides, what is there to see?"

"I'll be met by a guard. Just like any criminal. I'd rather she didn't see that," he says. He turns to me. "Elaine, you know what? I tried to tell Emily a little bit about me tonight. She wouldn't believe me. I mean, she acted like it was impossible. Like she couldn't be walking down the beach with a guy who stole a car. So, presto! I didn't do it. In her mind, I am your average school dropout who needs a little encouragement to become president of the United States." He shakes his head. Dark curls fall on his forehead. He pushes them back.

At first I couldn't see why Emily fell for Troy. But now, looking at him . . . I can. There is something innocent about the guy. His eyes simmer with a kind of protesting dignity. Even when he is reminding me that he is guilty of stealing a car.

Emily walks up to us. "It looks nice in there. So clean," she says.

She puts her hand in Troy's.

"I am going to figure out a way to see you again, soon," she says.

This is news to me. Emily won't have another chance to come back here until spring break.

Troy looks away.

"Aren't you glad?" she asks him.

"I tried to tell you something tonight. I wanted you to know the worst about me. But you wouldn't believe me so I had to stop." His voice is angry. "I don't think we should see each other any more."

Emily draws back. "Didn't you have a good time tonight?"

Troy flings himself away from her, shaking his head.

"Listen to this, Emily. I stole a car. Nod if you get that."

Emily doesn't nod. Finally, she gives a little duck to her head.

"Okay. Now, I'd like to tell you why." The guy heaves a big sigh and then says, "I was tapped to join a neighborhood gang in Oakland. I didn't want to join. When you get to be a homeboy, you have to kill people. We moved to San Francisco, but the homeboys, that's what we call gang members, followed me and . . . I'd be dead if I refused to join the second time I was asked. Have you got that?"

Emily ducks her head again.

"My initiation was to steal a car. I didn't want to do it. I was glad when I was caught." He stops. Slowly, he says, "Stealing a car is a felony. I was seventeen at the time. If I'd been eighteen, I might be in jail. I'm safe in Juvenile Hall. I don't want to leave. So don't talk about all these things I can do when I get out."

My twin has become as still as a stone. I can hear her breathe. It seems like years go by. After a long, long time, she holds out her arms. Troy pulls her to him. I feel like a dirty old peeping Tom but I watch. It makes my heart flop over.

Mama comes up to us, takes a look at Troy and Emily, who are still kissing . . . this is one of the longest kisses the world has ever known. Mama scowls at them. She gets in the car. In a minute, she honks the horn. The lovebirds fly apart and look around, dazed.

Everybody is laughing as we drive away.

Emily looks back until Troy disappears inside Juvenile Hall. Then my twin lunges against me and gives me a giant hug. We are on the backseat and Mama, who is chauffeuring us, laughs at us in the rearview mirror.

"That was fun," Mama says. "You had a good time, didn't you dear? Not you, Elaine. I am talking to Emily."

To whom it may concern, I had a good time, too.

"I had a wonderful time. Thanks, Mama," Emily says.

Mama smiles and turns on the car radio to her favorite country and western station and a male voice sings out, "Hello Trouble." She turns it up so we can hear it, too. I wish she would deprive us now and then.

Emily lunges against me again. Do I deserve this much affection?

But this time, she whispers in my ear.

"You've got to help me, Elaine."

"The last time you said that it got me in trouble," I tell her.

"This won't. All I want is for you to help me talk Mama and Dad into letting me come out here a few days during the Christmas holidays."

"But I'm going . . ." I begin. Emily clamps her hand over my mouth and I realize I am shouting. I whisper, "But I'm going to see you and Dad. I need some time with our father, just like you needed this time out here with our mother. Why should I change my plans to suit you?"

"You won't have to. I want you to come to see me and Dad. Just go home a little early and I'll go with you. All we have to do is stick together on this one and our parents will agree. Okay?"

Is this woman selfish or what?

I glare at her.

"And what if I don't want to leave early?" I demand.

"Are you selfish or what?" she cries out loud. She gasps when Mama swings her head around. "We're just goofing off," Emily tells her.

My twin turns back to me, gives me a long-gone, beat-down look, and moves away over to her corner of the backseat. She folds her hands in her lap like some little kid who got a scolding.

"Oh, all right," I mutter, "but no more than two days. That's three counting the flight out. Don't ask me to give up more than three days."

She flashes that big smile in the dark of the car. She grips my arm and shakes me. I guess she is saying, "Thank you, you extraordinary woman, you gorgeous girl of my dreams. I pledge my lifelong servitude to your every whim." Don't I wish!

What she actually says is, "Oh, Elaine! Oh, Elaine! Oh, Elaine!" Not nearly as good as pledging her lifelong servitude, but the feeling she puts into it! The inside of my chest is one big hunk of melting butter. I flash my big, matching smile back at her.

The car stops. We are home. We both tear into the house at the sound of the telephone.

Emily gets there first.

"Is that you, Mother? Yeah, on Flight 249, Gate 33. Eight o'clock, I think." She fishes something out of her purse. "Five after eight. Yeah, I'm having a wonderful time. Of course I miss you! I love you, too. What about Elaine? Sure. She's right here." Emily hands the telephone to me. We exchange a puzzled look.

"Hello Kay," I say. Kay is Emily's stepmother.

"I have a suggestion," she tells me. Her voice, a fruity, Julia Child kind of voice, brings her face back and I see her in my mind's eyes. A tall woman, not fat but big-boned. Not pretty but handsome. A little bossy. With Emily, a lot bossy. I can't stand the way she tells my twin what to wear and how to fix her hair. The interior decorator . . . that's Kay . . . wants to adjust everybody's appearance to coordinate with her favorite colors. It is her business to alter the appearance of things and she is good at it. And she is not mean. Actually, she is not so bad once you let her know you are not a helpless child.

"I've got a great idea," she warbles into my ear. "I think you are going to like it." She pauses.

"Shoot," I say.

"Why don't you invite Dean to meet you here for the Christmas holidays? Wouldn't that be fun! I don't know how you would get much time with him if you had to travel up to see him and then come back here to spend Christmas with us, do you? Am I making sense?"

"Oh, Kay!" I love this woman. "How wonderful!" I can't believe I am going to get to spend all my holidays with Dean as well as with Dad. "Can Dean be there when I get there? Can he stay till I leave?" She barely has time to say "Yes" before I go on, "You are so nice to think of Dean and me. How can I ever thank you . . . ?"

Not until I am hanging up the telephone do I remember something.

I told Emily I would give up three days of my Florida vacation. But I didn't know then, did I, that I would be giving up three days with Dean? She can't ask me to do that.

I turn around to go look for her, but she is right behind me.

Emily's blue eyes are icy.

I was feeling soft as a cloud inside, but now I scowl . . . I can feel my happy mood changing, fast.

Neither of us says anything. All at once, Emily turns her back on me and marches to our bedroom. I hear the door close.

Mama is in her bedroom undressing. I start toward her door. And stop. This is not one for her to solve. Emily and I have got to handle this ourselves.

I have known my twin for only a short time. After we got together in Florida, we started writing to each other. We wrote about all kinds of things, our parents and our boyfriends included. When our letters crossed they would be about the same person or about the same feelings. It was eerie how much alike we seemed to be. So I thought this visit from Emily would be just one long week of getting along. But it hasn't been that way.

I think back. Emily is a bathroom hog, no question. Same with her clothes. She doesn't like me to wear them. Even when I ask and she says "Yes," I can tell she hates it. And she doesn't like to hear me talk about our dad. Is she jealous and stingy? Bingo!

A small voice in the back of my head says, "But . . ."

Okay. Maybe there are things she doesn't like about me, too. I used to think I was almost perfect, but acquiring a sister changed that.

I am insensitive, she says. She says I don't

care what she thinks. And that I always make
the plans before she can open her mouth.

I wonder if she feels like I do? That getting
to know somebody up close is different from
long-distance knowing? And a lot harder.

Talk about hard love. It isn't easy to love my
twin. Of course I can't hold back my feelings
for her when she cries about being homesick.
Or when she gets lovesick over Troy. Or when
she grabs my arm and says I have to help her
get in trouble. I can't help loving the way she
needs me. And even though it is hard to love
her at other times, I wouldn't change us. We
aren't perfect together, but we are very important to each other.

My feet head for the closed door. I am almost
there when the door opens and Emily's head
pops out.

"I'm sorry," we say together.

We gasp. Then we begin to smile and Emily
says, "So . . . we're okay?"

I reach out and touch her hand. We are a
little embarrassed.

"Friends?" I ask.

"Friends," she says.

We stand there looking at the floor and smiling.

"You don't have to come back here with me.
After Christmas day, I'll tell my stepmother
and Dad that I am going to California alone for
a couple of days. I mean, it's time I started be-

ing up front with my parents. Telling them what I want to do." Her chin is up.

I have never seen her like this. So . . . real-womanlike. What is happening to Emily-the-little-girl?

"Sounds good to me. But if you get into trouble, I'll speak up. Just to let them know I am on your side." I say.

"Thanks, Elaine. I could do it alone, but I feel stronger when you and I stick together."

CHAPTER FIVE
Emily

It is a long way home even by plane. What can you do besides sit?

I walk up the aisle to the magazine rack. *Sports Illustrated. Newsweek. Life.* There is nothing here for a teenager to read. Aren't we people, too?

I know I am being grumpy.

I hated leaving Troy and I am going to miss Mama and Elaine.

Elaine.

What happens to Elaine and me? I never fought this way with a friend. Of course, Elaine is more than a friend. We are already so close it is eerie. When she is near I don't want to do anything without her. But she can be humongously stupid.

Like a couple of days ago. She returned my best shirt with blueberry yogurt spilled down the front. There were little bits of blueberries still stuck to the cloth. All she said was, "I looked great in it, didn't I?" My skin burns right now when I think about how mad that made me.

While I am on the subject, how about the way she talks about Dad? Incessantly. Like he is not just an everyday person who gets bran flakes stuck between his teeth.

To Elaine, our father is the king of the mountain. There's been nothing like him since the world began. The fact that he's got a nineteenth-century tongue that makes him say things like "albeit" and "be that as it may" and "greater love hath no man" and "casting pearls before swine" and—here's a real beauty—"whithersoever" . . . the fact that he talks this way makes her swoon with admiration.

I can't watch it. The two of them and their mutual admiration society! It's sick.

In fact, I am dreading what I know is going to happen. The minute I step off this plane, Dad is going to ask about Elaine. Not me. Elaine. Wait and see, I tell myself.

I haven't got long to wait now, and soon we are above Orlando. There is a sunset that has turned the whole sky red. For a second, I realize how much I love this part of Florida. Middle Florida, with its hills and lakes. Sometimes I think that all the trees left in the state are in the middle. And Fern, my little hometown, is nestled among the prettiest hills and lakes and trees of them all. Of course Fern, which is about forty miles from Orlando, doesn't have an airport, so the parents have to meet me here.

We are on the ground and in a few minutes I am rushing up the ramp into the lounge.

There they are. My white-haired father who walks straight-backed like his tall father (only on Dad, who is short, this straight-backed walk looks stiff) and my stepmother, who stands beside him. They both give me killer smiles and wave like they are hailing a taxi. I steel myself. I can take it, I can take it, I say over and over. Albeit and howsoever I know I may hate it, I can take it.

Smack! It hits me. All this agonizing, fearful, clinging, nervous parent-love. Arms go around me. I am smothered between them. They say they have missed me so much it nearly killed them. But I am still alive. I am still breathing. I survived this ungodly separation and I came back to them. From now on, total happiness! From now on, us, us, us. Us, the perfect family, together again!

It is a gruesome experience, but I do and say everything I am supposed to do and say. It isn't hard. I just push the button and it rolls out.

I am in the car, squeezed in between them. Mother is driving. She is a good driver but I don't relax. I am waiting for . . .

"How was Elaine?" Dad asks.

"Fine," I say. Let's see what he does with that.

"I am glad to hear it. And your mother?"

He doesn't fool me. Asking about Mama isn't going to change the subject.

"She's fine, too." I can see her face, right now. "She teaches a sort of therapy class for first offenders and it is really neat—" I get interrupted.

"Is Elaine coming for Christmas?" he asks. Before I can answer, he says, "She said she would try to come, but I am not confident that she really wants to. I think she has a wrong impression of Fern. She seems to think it is just another little cow town. We must help her see that this is her town. She was born here. Her ancestors were born here. The place was named for her grandmother who, by the way, was tall like you two girls. The more Elaine understands about our family, a family that pioneered this small part of the country, the more she will want to take her place as a member of the Petty family. Which is her rightful place in the world. There are a lot of things you can do to insure this, Emily. Albeit a challenge, it should be a happy one. Can I count on you?"

I punch the button and say, "Of course." I punch it again because I feel I must say more, but nothing comes out. Then my mouth opens and my tongue starts speaking for the real me. "I don't see why . . ." Dad turns his tiny, brilliant blue eyes on me. I stop and start again. "It isn't up to me, Dad. Whether or not Elaine likes Fern, well, that is up to her, isn't it?" I am gaining momentum. "And if it means a lot to you, maybe you should—" Again, I am interrupted.

Kay, the kindly person who raised me, the person I call Mother, says, "Elaine is coming, Wesley. I made sure of that. I spoke to her last night on the telephone. I told her to invite her beau. She will have so much fun she will want to come back as often as you want her to. Now stop worrying about it. We've got one chick back and we are nearly home so let's celebrate. How does a cup of hot chocolate sound?"

She gives me a quick glance between oncoming cars. It is a secretive glance. With her black eyebrows raised and her lips turned up in a small smile, I know she means for me to feel her support. We both love Dad, but there are times when we have to give each other some backup against his decision-making attacks. If he could, he would make everybody's decisions for them and expect the "thank you's" to roll in.

But this time I wish she hadn't interrupted me. Actually, I wish she wouldn't always jump in and try to smooth things over with her hot chocolate or whatever.

What am I saying? Mother has saved my bacon a lot of times by diverting Dad. I appreciate it. But do I see something else going on? It is almost as though Mother thinks of herself as the great peacemaker. Like it is up to her to keep Dad and me from talking about anything important enough to make us mad at each other. I need to talk to my father. Maybe I need to get mad at him sometimes. What is she afraid of? That Dad and I will tear each other apart? Or, worse still, that we will work things out without her help?

I shrink down in the seat trying to get away from both parents.

The car pulls into the driveway.

This is not your ordinary driveway. It is half a block long and it winds through a walled garden. As you come through the ancient oak trees all dripping with moss just like on the postcards, the columned Southern mansion heaves into view. It is a big house for three people. Why have I never thought about this before? Maybe I am remembering Mama's little house in California. I liked that little house. And Elaine loved this big one.

Elaine practically lived in my jacuzzi. She knows how to enjoy the scene but she doesn't know what it's like to live in the biggest house in town all your life. I got teased about it when I was a kid.

My muscular father insists on carrying my suitcase inside. While Mother pours the hot chocolate, I open the suitcase and give them the presents I bought them. Aztec cuff links for Dad and a matching brooch for Mother. I guess I think of them as kind of like twins, too.

At last, I get to go to my room. The first thing I do is call Michelle.

Michelle is my lifelong best friend. We grew up together because my Mother and Michelle's mother are best friends. Michelle is now the most beautiful girl in Fern. She is the reigning queen of everything. Just last summer, she was elected Citrus Queen and rode on the county float in the local Pioneer Festival parade. The good part was that she had to share the float with bushels of oranges. And she had to follow another float with two real live grunting, squealing pigs. All that blond beauty was less important to this farming community than the products of its labor!

"Hello, ugly," I say.

"Emily! You're back! Can I come over?" she asks.

"No. I'm in bed. Today went on forever." I take a deep breath and ask, "What's happening?"

"I think Kyle is going to disintegrate if he doesn't see you real quick. He was over here today moaning about you, saying how it's been a week and seems like a year. Isn't that sweet? The guy has really changed from the nerd we used to know."

"I've got a lot to tell you, Michelle," I murmur darkly. "But it will have to wait until tomorrow." We hang up. I think about what she said. How much Kyle, which rhymes with bile, has changed.

Has Kyle changed? Is he sweet? Any guy might look good beside Michelle's Neanderthal. Broderick, that is.

This is heavy thinking. Like Scarlett, I think I better put it off now and pick up on it tomorrow.

But first, I call Kyle.

"Hi," I say.

"Emily? Is that you? You sound different," he says.

I am, I am. But I don't say this.

"I missed you. Really. It seemed like you were gone forever." He pauses. I don't say anything. "So I have to see you, kid. There's a party at Broderick's tomorrow night. When should I pick you up?"

Another silence. I have to say something.

"I don't know. I mean, I don't know if I am going." This is ridiculous. All my friends will be at Broderick's party. I want to go. It would be crazy to stay home. But with Kyle?

But, of course with Kyle. I have to see him to tell him about Troy. I'll go to the party with him and tell him sometime during the evening.

"What do you mean?" he asks.

"Nothing. Pick me up around eight. Okay?"

Has it only been a week since I saw Kyle? When he arrives, I take a second look. I knew he was growing taller. He was never fat, but I hadn't noticed how lean he is becoming. Was his hair like that when I left? It grows down his neck in back and is short on top. I think the short-on-top is new. As we drive out to Broderick's I keep sneaking peeks at my date. No question, Kyle has potential.

We are both in a quiet mood, but that changes when we get to Broderick's. The guy lives on a lake and the party is on the beach. Everybody I know is there, even the Mexican kids that Broderick used to hate. Raul, who calls himself "Scurvy Dog," and his girlfriend, Ilda. Broderick is running for class president and wants their votes.

Ilda comes up and hugs me. Then Michelle. Broderick gives me a salute from the buffet table where he is munching down on corn dogs. I forget about Kyle and start telling the gang about California. That faraway place that haunts our small-town dreams. Then we hear water splashing. We all run down to the edge of the lake and watch some kids in two canoes jousting with paddles. Kyle comes up beside me just as one kid goes in the water.

Kyle and I grab hands and laugh like fools. We lead the way to the dock and yell at the guy in the water. Kyle bends over to help him crawl up on the deck. I am holding Kyle around the waist. The guy heaves halfway out of the water, grabs Kyle by the leg, and pulls him in. I go in with him.

It is November and the water is icy. I shoot up and gasp for air. To my amazement, I see several more of the guys jumping off the dock. Then a couple of the girls take a dive. Raul and Ilda jump in together. We all go under and come up, screaming with laughter. I look toward the beach. The whole crowd has run to the water's edge to watch us. Some of the kids wade out and swim toward us. I never had so much fun in my life.

I was freezing at first but now I am tingling warm all over. My clothes billow around me like soggy balloons.

Kyle and I are swimming in place and spewing water like a couple of whales. The kids closest to us start doing it, too, and soon we have a fountain going. We choke, we cough, we spew. We aim at the cautious kids who are still on the dock. We miss most of them, but we get some water on a few. I go under for another mouthful. When I come up, Kyle comes up beside me. His face, cheeks bulging, is next to mine. Somebody behind me bumps into me and I am squashed against Kyle. He spews like a papa whale. He shoots a fountain straight up in the air and it comes down on his head. I laugh so much I can't talk. I grab him around the neck and shake him.

Then we kiss each other, hard. We hold each other tightly. It feels so good I can't stop. Softly we go down in the water to chin level and rest there. My hair is all over his face and a piece of it is between us just missing our lips. I pull back to move it out of the way and start to kiss him again when I come to my senses.

"Don't stop now," he says.

I look around. We are the only people left in the water. How embarrassing.

"We've got to get out," I say, starting to swim toward the shore.

I can hear him behind me.

On the beach all the wet kids are circling a torch to dry out. Broderick's dad has lighted the place up until it is as bright as day. There are real flames coming out of the stakes. They are everywhere. Kyle and I huddle close to one.

I bend over to dry my hair. I feel his hand run through the wet stuff as he tries to untangle it.

"I missed your hair," he says. "Even when it's slimy wet, it's still beautiful."

"I'll leave it with you next time I go," I tell him

"Seriously. Life as we know it in Fern, Florida isn't the same without you, Emily. I'm glad my significant other is back."

"We've got to talk," I say.

Somebody is ringing a cowbell. It is deafening. Everybody gets quiet.

The announcer, Broderick, says, "The band is here. Let's dance." He puts the bell down and leads the crowd toward the lighted tennis court. I hear a drum, then an electric guitar. Then the night bursts open with sound.

Kyle and I still look bedraggled but we are mostly dry. We are dancing before we get to the courts. I find that my damp hair slings back better than when it is dry. I am slinging from side to side and over my head and down in front and back. I whack everybody within slinging distance.

The music never stops but we take a rest. Panting like a pair of marathon runners, we go over and sit beside Michelle. Michelle, the poor, gorgeous thing, broke her toe and is wearing a shoe with a cutout so the toe can stick out and breathe. I love how she broke it. According to Kyle, she was playing croquet last week and whacked her foot with her own mallet. You've got to love somebody like that.

"I wish I could dance," she moans. She gives us a pity-me look.

Broderick comes over and flops in a chair beside Michelle.

"Did you guys get some of the barbecue? Put lots of sauce over it. Ymm, yum." He licks his lips. "You know what? I could eat some more. Be a good girl and get me some, will you, Michelle?"

Obediently, Michelle gets up and starts limping off toward the buffet table. I see her stop. She turns around and comes back.

"Get it yourself." She sits down.

"Aw, come on. Give me a break. Don't play these women-libber games, Michelle. I'd do the same thing for you if I hadn't just danced my feet off." He raises his feet and lowers them with a sigh.

Michelle looks at me. She looks at Kyle.

"You'd never ask Emily to go get your food for you, would you, Kyle?" she says. She gives him a long look of frank admiration.

Kyle squirms uncomfortably. Michelle has never really looked at him before.

"Emily wouldn't do it. So what's the use of asking?" He turns to Broderick and laughs. It is a high, insincere laugh. I know Broderick is not one of his favorite people.

"There. See. Emily wouldn't. I won't either." Michelle settles back in her chair and turns to watch the dancers. She is stiff as a poker.

"Aw." Broderick gets up, kicks some sand around, and goes off to the buffet table alone.

In a low voice, Michelle says to me, "I never realized how lucky you were to have a guy like Kyle."

"Excuse us, Michelle. I've got to talk to Kyle, alone." I get up. Kyle gets up, looking surprised and puzzled. We walk off.

"I've got something to tell you, Kyle," I say, and proceed not to tell him. A couple of minutes later, he is still waiting. Finally, I say, "I met someone." When those words hit the air, they sound so wrong I wish I could take them back.

Kyle repeats after me. "You met someone?" He shakes his head in wonder. "Wasn't that me you were kissing a few minutes ago?"

I don't say anything.

His face changes. He goes from puzzled to squint-eyed.

"When I picked you up tonight, I noticed something. You were different. If you don't count that imaginary kiss, the one I imagined we had out there in the lake . . . I have to admit I did feel something different. Like you had changed." He pauses and shifts from one foot to the other. He looks away and back at me. "Somebody you met in Corte Madera?"

"Close. San Francisco. I met him in San Francisco."

"Let's go home, okay?" he says. I nod.

I go to tell Michelle good-bye. I say something polite to Broderick about how good his party was. The two are sitting together looking grumpy. Broderick is munching on barbecue from a huge platter. Through a full mouth he says, "It's early."

"Yeah," Michelle says, "what's your hurry?"

"It's me. I'm still pooped from the trip," I say.

"In that case"—she twists toward Kyle, who is standing to one side—"why don't you come back, Kyle? I'd like the company. It gets lonely here on the sidelines. Would you be interested in watching with me?"

Kyle throws out his hands in a disinterested way. Then he looks at Michelle again. Beautiful Michelle. Who is looking up at him in that practiced way she has. Somehow she manages to look like poor-little-me and watch-out-for-the-blond-bombshell at the same time. How does she do that?

"Maybe I will," Kyle says.

CHAPTER SIX
Elaine

I'm awesome!

It is the first day of Christmas holidays and I am on my way to Florida. Last week, I told my friend Nita that I couldn't go to Florida looking like my ordinary self. "Help!" I said. She went with me to all the local resale stores. We found some super stuff and some of it is on me right now.

The plane is easing down over Orlando. It rolls to the ground, and the minute it comes to a stop I am up. I hang my duffel bag over a shoulder and straighten my blazer. My *great* blazer!

When Nita spotted this black jacket, it wasn't all that great. I had to cut off the bottom and sew on a long, thin narrow scarf. A black, see-through thing. Now, with the blazer buttoned, the gold chain of my pocket watch glitters right through it. That gets a lot of second looks. Of course, I can't be sure but what people are staring at my argyle vest, my striped trousers, my newsboy cap, or my reverse saddle shoes. The only thing on me that's not second-hand is those shoes. I had to go to a men's store to find them.

Reverse saddle shoes? Okay, that means they are brown from the sole up about halfway, then white. Devastating!

Emily is going to panic with envy. She won't find anything like these shoes in Fern.

I am coming off the ramp into the boarding lounge. The family will be there. Dad, Kay, and my twin. And Dean.

I met Dean in Fern last summer when I came with Mama to see Emily. He is tall and blond and good-looking. We look classic together. I really liked him right away. But two weeks didn't give us much time together. Now, maybe I can get to know him.

I wish I could stop here in the ramp and look in my mirror, but I am pushed along in the crowd. I know my hair shines like tinsel because I put hairshine on it just before we landed. And I know my lips look moist because . . . oops, here we are.

I reach up and tip my newsboy cap at a sassy angle as I step off the ramp and into the lounge.

The first person I see is Dean. I didn't remember that he was soooo outstanding! I can't believe he is mine! How did I get so lucky?

He sees me and we both grin like hyenas. I run through the crowd toward Dean, but Kay and Dad intercept me. I get hugged, but I look over Dad's shoulder at Dean. He walks up close, bends over Dad's shoulder, and gives me a warm, wonderful peck.

Then I see Emily. I haven't seen her since she visited me in California at fall break. I get loose from everybody and grab her. It's like I'm the magic prince that awakens the sleeping princess. She begins to smile, then laugh. We hop up and down and she takes my cap and puts it on her head.

"Where did you get it? I've got to have it," she cries.

"It's yours," I say. My hair got messed up in the grab but I don't care. Dean is on one side of me and Emily is on the other. Let me die and go to heaven, right now. Things can't get better than this.

Everybody talks at once. Nobody remembers how to get back to Dad's car. Dean, of course, spots it. He takes Kay's arm and leads her to the passenger side, opens the door and ushers her in. She beams. I can see that she is charmed out of her wits. She smiles out at me approvingly. I feel like she is saying, "I like you better already. You chose well." I am grinning all over with pride.

Then Dean opens the back door for Emily. He packs her inside, then runs back around the car to open the door for me. I have to smile because it seems a little too busy, a little too much like a staged exercise in an old movie. I mean I feel like I have to stand still and wait until he can get to me. Then I remember.

Although Dean goes to school in New England, he is from South Carolina. I think that, for him, all these good manners are not just for show. My grandfather is from South Carolina and he is overflowing with good manners. He really cares for people, and treating them with consideration comes naturally to him.

It is soooo nice to see Dean acting like he really cares for others. It makes me love him more.

All the way to Fern, Dean tells Emily and me about his first semester at Crown University. No book talk. Not much sports talk. If I had to name it, I'd say it was girl talk.

"You've got all the girl you can handle," I interrupt, pointing to myself.

He stops midsentence. "You know, you're right." I get kissed, again.

When we get to Dad's house, Emily takes me to her bedroom where I will bunk. In this big house I could have a room to myself, but we agreed to stay together in her bedroom so we can talk at night. Now, the first thing I want to talk to my twin about is a delicate matter. I ask her for all the local news, but she knows I mean . . . what about Kyle and Michelle? She wrote me last week that they are dating. You'd think she would be glad to get Kyle out of her hair considering how nuts she is about Troy. But it isn't working that way.

Emily throws herself across the bed and watches me unpack. Mournfully she says, "Everywhere I go, I see them. Always together.

Holding hands. Rubbing shoulders. They act so mushy I can't stand it."

"But, Emily . . ." I begin.

"Don't say it. I don't know why I feel this way. Maybe if I could hear from Troy it would help."

"Doesn't he write?" I ask.

"Hardly ever. I wish I could call him."

"You can. His restrictions have been lifted for good behavior," I say, sitting beside her. I can hang up my clothes later. This is an emergency. I hand her the telephone.

Her eyes get big. "You mean right now?" she asks.

I open my address book and find the number and hand it to her.

She dials. "Oh, good grief. What time is it in California?" She looks like she is about to panic.

I look at my watch. It is three in the afternoon here. That makes it close to noon back home, I tell her. But she isn't listening anymore. Somebody is on the other end of the line. She asks to speak to Troy. She waits. Then smiles.

"Is that you, Troy?" she says. Then her brow creases. I can't tell what he is saying but it must not be good. She doesn't say a word for a long time. Then she says, "I'm sorry. I am so sorry." Finally, she says, "I'll call you back in a little while, okay? Yeah, I've got an idea that may help." Then she hangs up.

"What's the biggest worry Dean has, Elaine?" she asks slowly.

I am surprised by the question. I think about it.

"How many parties he can work into a weekend," I say, laughing.

Emily nods. "Know what Troy's is?" She lets the question hang there for a second then answers it. "What his old neighborhood gang is going to do to him when he gets out. He is going to be released soon. His probation officer has found a place for him in a foster home in Oakland. Oakland is where he got in trouble. That's where his gang hangs out. They didn't like it when he got caught. Get the picture?"

"That's terrible," I murmur.

We sit there silent for a few minutes.

"I don't think I am going out to California next week after all," she says.

"But you were counting on it," I say.

She waits a second then says, "He doesn't want me to come, Elaine. What can I do?" She begins to cry.

Some Christmas this is going to be!

I put my arms around her.

Her head is down. She looks up at me. "Will you go with me out to the old family farmhouse sometime while you are here? Remember the old farmhouse? The house where we were born."

"I'd love to. Can we do it this afternoon? Dean would enjoy that."

"When you and I go, I want us to go alone," she says, getting up.

"That makes it harder. I can't just go off and leave Dean the first day he is here. But some day soon I'll work something out so . . . so we can do it your way," I say.

Emily gives me a funny look and says, "Forget it. Really. It's okay."

"Are you sure?" I ask.

She nods.

I don't see much of my twin for the next few days. Dean and I are home every evening because Dad asked us to have dinner each night with the family, but I don't get a chance to talk to Emily at dinner.

Dad can't get enough of me. He wants to know every detail of my life. He wants the history of every year that he and I have been separated. I have learned to sit close to him so we aren't yelling across the big table.

Kay watches us with a smile. Emily watches us with a look of disgust. She yawns and stretches. She interrupts. Is she jealous or what? Doesn't she know that Dad and I just want to get to know each other? After all, she has Dad to herself all day because Dean and I drive off and see the sights.

Dean rented a little car soon after he arrived and we spend every day chasing around from the east coast to walk beside the Atlantic to the west coast for a dip in the warm gulf. Dean likes it when we go swimming. He can't believe my great body in a bathing suit.

Today we plan to spend the whole day roaming a deserted campus. Rollins College is a pretty school nestled among lakes and hills. Dean has this idea that we should both go to Rollins in a couple of years.

We get to the campus and walk it over. All the college kids have gone home for Christmas so we have it to ourselves. After an hour, we find a piece of green grass beside a lake where we eat the sandwiches we packed this morning. When we finish, we watch some kids trying to make a sailboat take off, but the breeze is as soft as a butterfly flap. It doesn't work. The kids wade ashore and dock the sailboat and study the sky. No clouds. We can't help but laugh.

I feel so grown up with Dean. These kids with the sailboat look about sixteen, my age. But with an eighteen-year-old college guy beside me, I feel a hundred years older than the sailors. It is a new kind of feeling and I like it.

"We ought to start thinking about the future," Dean says. He points across the lake. "See that row of buildings. Those are off-campus apartments for students. Isn't that neat?"

I agree.

Dean takes my hand in his. "If we were going to school here, we could get one of those apartments. We wouldn't have to live in a stuffy dormitory. That kind of living is for the nerds. Every normal person on my campus lives in an apartment."

I have the feeling I missed something.

"What?" I ask.

"You heard me," he says.

"Aren't you taking a lot for granted?" I ask. We are smiling at each other in a teasing way.

"Come on, Elaine. It's the only way to go." A little impatiently, Dean gets up and pulls me to my feet. We start walking away from the water. "Someday when you grow up you will agree with me. I just hope I am still around to reap the benefits."

I grab his hand and pull him to a stop. I am one of these people who has to know what is going on. And right now.

"I don't want to have sex with anybody, yet," I say. It is like a trick question. I watch him to see how he will respond.

He looks me up and down. He isn't smiling, now.

With one rough jerk, he pulls me against him. He kisses me. In the daylight. In public. Somebody walks by. A man with a dog.

We come apart. But I am still feeling kissed. It feels wonderful. I don't want to quarrel. Is that what we were doing?

"You love me, don't you?" he asks. I nod. "That makes sex . . . all right." He tilts my chin up. "Elaine, I've been looking forward to this holiday. For a special reason. I want you. And you know you want me to make love to you. Can't we get away from the family, tonight? Isn't there somewhere we can go for a little privacy?"

"You want to make love to me? I always

hated that way of putting it. It sounds like the woman just lies there and gets something done to her." I know I am stalling.

Dean looks unhappy. "You don't have to turn it into a competitive sport." He drops my hand.

"Okay. Let's talk about our future, as you put it." I hate it when I get nervous and talkative but I can't stop. "If we start having sex, I could get pregnant. I might not be able to go to college, not if I had a baby." I am quoting from a book I read. Something tells me that I sound like I am quoting from a book I read.

"Oh, great!" he says to himself, rolling his eyes. "We might as well go back to the car." He starts off ahead of me.

I catch up with him.

"But it does happen, doesn't it?" Why won't he listen to me? I know I sound childish. Panicked. But shouldn't he listen to me? He turns abruptly and I almost run into him.

"You can't be serious," he chides. "You don't believe those old scare tactics do you? About how the girl gets pregnant and the couple lives miserably ever after? Do you actually believe everything you read? That is so dumb." He turns away. "I don't know how I ever got mixed up with a person your age, anyway."

Immediately he turns back to me. "I'm sorry, Elaine. It's just that you are spoiling things for us. It doesn't need to be this way. We had a good thing going. You are a beautiful girl. I love you. Everything I have suggested has been because I love you."

That is sweet!

He comes close to me and I put my head on his chest and just rest a minute. This feels so good I wish it could go on forever.

"Dean," I whisper.

"Yes, darling?" he says.

"If you love me so much . . . then you don't want me to do something I don't want to do, right?"

"Of course not. But you see, Elaine, you don't know what you really want until you sample it. I can tell"—he says this gently—"you don't know much about sex. Not to worry. You love me. That's all you need to know. Leave the rest to me."

I draw back.

"Which means you do know something about sex?"

He laughs. "Every eighteen-year-old guy knows something about sex. Let me demonstrate."

Holding my hand, Dean leads me to a cluster of trees. Inside this circle of trees it is so dark it looks like twilight. I feel as though we are enclosed by walls of greenery. A minute later . . . I don't know how it happened . . . Dean and I are lying on a thick mat of fallen leaves. This is when I realize what he meant when he said "Let me demonstrate." He definitely knows how to kiss! At first he is so sweet, so gentle! Each time he kisses me, I hold him close. When he draws back to say he loves me, I put my lips against his face. The touch of his fingers on my

neck . . . he pulls my collar down to kiss my
shoulder . . . how can his touch make me feel
so good? This flood of happiness . . . I am thinking this is the real thing. His hand goes under
my shirt and explores my bare back. I feel him
unsnap my bra. I go stiff. I try to say something. But he is kissing me. I try to push away,
but he is heavy and strong. For a few seconds,
I don't realize . . . that something has changed!
Dean is holding me down. He is trying to force
me.

I twist my head to one side to break away
from his kiss. When did he get rough? I say,
"Don't, Dean. I told you I didn't want to." I am
trying to hold his hand. He is touching my
body, roughly. Hurting me. He is handling me
as though I am a thing . . . a thing that belongs
to him.

"Listen!" I yell. "I don't want to. I told
you. . . ."

"You didn't mean that," he says. His voice
is angry, flat.

"I do," I say. I am crying, trying to sit up.
He pushes me back on the ground. I hate his
kiss this time. It doesn't have any love in it.
And we aren't kissing to please me. Just him.
He is trying to do something to me, not with
me. And he will be mad if I don't let him. He
may be really mad and not like me anymore.
For a second I go limp and let the tears flow. I
hear him mutter, "That's the way. Just relax."

Then I go stiff as a poker. With all my
strength, I shove Dean off of me and sit up.

This knocks him backward. I pull the neck of my blouse up and stare at him. He sits up and stares back. He looks surprised.

In a second he turns red. We keep glaring at each other as I straighten my clothes. I start to say something but my voice comes out in a hiss.

"I haven't had sex yet. And I don't want to have sex yet. And I don't want somebody else telling me that I do want to or should want to if I don't want to. When I have sex it will be because I have decided to myself. Based on my own feelings, not somebody else's feelings." I hiss this out in a loud whisper.

"That's really dumb. Do you know how dumb that sounds?" Dean jumps to his feet shouting. What happened to his cool, grown-up manner?

I don't think I know this guy. I stand up, too, and shove my hands in my skirt pockets.

"I think I know your trouble. You are afraid of sex. Admit it, Elaine. You've never done it and you have these big, scary ideas about it. You act like a weirdo," he says. He leans against a tree and folds his arms. His cool is back.

"I am not afraid," I mutter. "Well, maybe I am. But no way can you make me think I am a weirdo. I know I will like sex at the right time with the right person."

He steps forward, smiles, and puts his hands on my shoulders.

"Are you saying I am not the right person?" His smile is taunting. Everything the guy is . . . a college guy, an eighteen-year-old, smart, cool, good-looking . . . says that he is the right person. But he tried to force me, didn't he?

Maybe he is going to try it again. I get nervous and start talking again.

"I don't believe everything I read in books, but . . . maybe you can explain this to me: I read somewhere that kids who ignore the 'scare tactics' are the ones who get AIDS. This book said that anybody who is careless just one time can get it. A lot of college kids are dying from it."

Dean swings his head from side to side impatiently.

"Give me credit, Elaine. I know all about that. I've fooled around and that was fun but that's over. From now on, I'm going to play it safe. I'm ready to settle down. With one, safe person. I had hoped that person would be you."

For one awful minute I freeze. Did he say what I think he said?

"But Dean, you may not be the safe person for me," I say slowly. "How do I know you haven't already been exposed to AIDS? You say you've been around. If you have been careless just once you could be carrying the virus. Right now." I catch my breath. There isn't enough air in the world to help me breathe easy while I am saying this. "Even if I wanted to have sex with you, I'd be crazy to take the chance, wouldn't I?"

Dean lifts his hands off my shoulders as if my skin is poison. His eyes turn cold. And, all at once, I see something else. He is more scared at this moment than I will ever be.

I look back on what just happened. He didn't argue. He didn't say he never got careless. So . . . did he?

He makes a big effort to look indifferent.

"Have it your way, Miss Know-It-All. You and your morals. I had you figured for a girl with some maturity. I was wrong. I don't know how we ever got together. You are a one-person lecture circuit."

I stand there gazing at this handsome blond guy. Who wouldn't fall for him? At the memory of how much I cared about him, I could cry. But what if we had had sex? At first, when he was loving and gentle, it wouldn't have been easy for me to say no. I get the shivers.

I know it is over. My heart is filled with jigsaw emotions. I am angry. But I am also sorry for Dean. I feel he has made some kind of mistake. Not just in losing me. That is too bad because I am not dumb and I am not a weirdo. I just won't do things his way. If he can't have sex with me, I know he doesn't want me for a friend and that hurts. But the biggest mistake Dean has made is about himself. Emily says Troy thinks of himself as a throwaway. I wouldn't bet on it. But Dean?

For all of this, I hear myself say, "I'm sorry."

"Oh, great!" he says. "Now she's sorry." He walks down the sidewalk to the parking lot. I follow. By the time we get to the car, tears flood my eyes again.

He looks at me. His old, sweet look. "I'm sorry, baby. But we just weren't meant to be. Please let's part peacefully. I hate scenes."

It is a long drive home. We don't talk. When we get there, Dean gets out, rushes around to my door, and opens it.

"I must speak to Kay," he says, following me inside. I wait in the living room.

He finds Kay in the kitchen. I hear him thanking her for her hospitality. Praising her generosity toward him. Complimenting her on her cooking. I close my ears.

Did I say Dean's manners were the real thing? I've got to rethink that one. Good manners mean real caring, don't they? Does Dean really care about others? I'm not sure. I still like good manners. But I am no longer impressed by this guy's show of politeness.

Soon he comes toward me carrying his overnight bag. He gives me one fierce, angry look then changes his face to a smile.

"It's been . . . surreal. Good-bye, baby." With a graceful swing of his shoulder, he pushes the door open and goes out. In a minute I hear his car start. Dean and I saw a lot of Florida in that little rented car. I thought we were having a wonderful time.

Now I am bawling. I run upstairs, looking for my twin. It will feel good to start talking. And talk and talk. Emily will listen and listen.

Maybe if I talk long enough, I will figure out what has happened and how I feel about it.

The bedroom is empty. Where is she?

I want to talk to my sister. No one else will do.

I wait.

Could she be at the old farmhouse? She wanted us to go there together but I never found the time.

I think that is where she is. I have a strong feeling about it. My twin-sense shoves into high gear and I run through the big, quiet house. In the garage, I look for Emily's bike. Just as I thought, it is gone. I jump on Kay's bike and head down the long driveway. You have to go a city block just to get out of this place.

Ten minutes later I turn in the little dirt driveway that leads up to the old farmhouse. It is a small house with only a couple of rooms downstairs and a couple more upstairs. The house where Mama and Dad lived with their two babies. The house where Mama lived on after Dad left. Those must have been sad times.

I come out of my reverie as I park my bike and walk up on the rickety old wooden porch. I reach for the doorknob. It begins to turn before I put my hand on it.

The door opens.

Troy stands on the other side!

"Where's your backpack?" he asks, looking around wildly.

"My backpack?"

"Didn't you get packed yet? What was the trouble? Too many people around? I'll bet every time you started out, you bumped into somebody, Elaine or your dad. Right? I thought so. Emily, we are going to have to wait until after dark." He fumbles around in his pocket and pulls out a fistful of bills.

"I counted this money you gave me and it's too much. It is about four times as much as we will need for two plane tickets to Mexico. Here." He tries to stuff it into my hands. I shove it back at him, protesting.

"No, don't give it to me. . . . " I say, loudly. What is going on?

He stops and studies me for a second. Our eyes meet. I am afraid that now is the moment he will recognize me. And, suddenly I don't want him to. Not until I know more. I duck my chin down like my twin does and concentrate, really hard, on looking like Emily. I can see in his eyes that he buys it.

He looks around and dumps all of those loose bills onto a table. Some of the bills drift to the floor.

"You must take it back. I have a feeling this is a special savings. College money, maybe." The guy looks over at me. His black eyebrows come together. "Maybe we are doing the wrong thing, Emily. I am not saying that just because getting married was your idea. But because your folks may hold it against you. I don't feel good about it. You want the truth, don't you? I feel lousy about it."

Getting married! My mouth drops open.

I must pull myself together.

"Then what did you want, Troy?" I ask. "What did you come here for?" I know I don't sound like Emily, but the guy is too upset to notice.

His eyes open wide. "You mean . . . what do you mean? You call me in California and I tell you I am going to be released. I say I have to run away. Then you say I've got to come here. Then I come. I spent half my running money for bus fare to come to Florida when I should have headed straight for Mexico. Now, please don't cry, Emily, but I have to tell you that I should be going on by myself. If I bring a wife like you, a redheaded half-breed, to my grandmother's house in Mexico . . . I don't know how she'll take it. Seriously." He looks at me pleadingly. "Why don't you wait here until we both know what we are doing? What's the rush? I love you, Emily. I'll keep on loving you as long as you want me to."

It is hard not to put my arms around Troy. Talk about a nice guy. Troy is the best.

But . . . my sister! Is she out of her mind?

Troy is still trying to reason with me. I mean with Emily. Anybody can see that the guy doesn't want to get married. Not tonight, anyway.

"What I really think, Emily, I think the best thing for me to do is . . . maybe I ought to head right back for San Francisco. I'd rather go to Mexico, of course, but if I go back to Juvenile

Hall they'll let me serve another term. I mean make me serve another term. For running away. I'd like that, you know. I'd be safe again. But you don't like it, do you?" He waits. I look confused. "Okay, let's talk about what is the best thing for you. You say you want to show your old man that he can't play favorites with Elaine and expect you to hang around and watch it? Do I have that right?"

I can't believe this. So this is what Emily tells people. Is this what she really thinks? I feel my face get hot. I can't help it, this makes me mad. I try to keep my mouth closed. I know if I say anything now, I'll blow my cover.

"I don't think this is a reason to get married," he says. "And another thing. If you run off without telling your old man, he may never trust you again. Think about it."

I mutter, "I'm thinking, Troy. Believe me, I'm thinking. I better go. The backpack, remember? I've got to sneak my backpack out of the house while everybody is at the dinner table. See you." I hurry outside before I get a sloppy lover's kiss. I run the bike down the road and hop on. I ride as fast as I can.

This twin-sense Emily and I share ... it worked. It told me she was at the old farmhouse and I just missed her. I let my mind go blank and wait for my twin-sense to work again. Where is Emily? I ask.

My bike comes off the dirt road onto pavement and I am riding into town. The wind blows into my face. I am turning down our street toward the house. Is Emily in her bedroom? Is she upstairs packing?

I wheel up the driveway and run upstairs. Emily is not there.

CHAPTER SEVEN
Emily

Every day this week my twin has gone somewhere with Dean. All I asked for was one hour alone with Elaine out at the old farmhouse where we were born. Just one hour.

I thought if we could go out there, just the two of us, we could have a real talk about Dad. Just being in that old house would help us get on the right track.

If you can't count on your twin, who can you count on?

I am flopped on the floor on my furry rug when a light bulb comes on in my head. Michelle! How could I forget Michelle? We've hardly seen each other since Elaine got here. Michelle is my lifelong best friend. I can't hold it against her that she is going with Kyle. I dumped him first, didn't I?

I call Michelle. She seems surprised to hear from me. I say, "Come over, you ugly thing." Her voice flies up. She wants to see me, she says. She's dying to see me. She'll come by immediately, but she can only stay a minute. I say okay. I know once I get her here I can make her stay.

In ten minutes I hear her running up the stairs. My door pops open.

"Emily!" She kneels beside me on the rug. Her amber hair streams down one side of her slender, perfect face. She seems aglow.

I know I look frumpy. But I don't care.

"So, how's the gang?" This is great. An old-fashioned, get-down, woman talk, just Michelle and me. I realize I am smiling when I feel my face muscles crack. My smile muscles haven't been taken out for exercise for quite a while.

"The old gang?" She sits back on her feet.

"Our friends. Broderick, Ilda, Raul . . . all the guys." Michelle can be retarded sometimes, but usually a nudge in the right direction snaps her out of it.

Both hands go up to her hair. She lifts it and drops it. I can see the wheels in her head turning. What now?

"I haven't seen anybody much lately," she says self-consciously.

"Why not? Did you die?"

She doesn't laugh.

She says, "I've been busy, you know. . . ." Slowly, she breathes out a big breath and crosses her arms. "You know what I mean."

Do I? Busy doing what? Then it comes to me. Is she trying to say that she is busy dating Kyle?

"Okay, okay. You can't date Kyle from

morning until night. So what have you been doing with the rest of your time?" I ask.

"But, I do. I mean we do. Kyle and I have been together every day this week. He's been taking me out to the barrio. He volunteers out there, you know. A huge load of books and toys for the Christmas party came in Monday and we've been unpacking ever since. Oh, Emily, I love to go out there with . . . to go out there. The little Mexican kids are adorable. I think the volunteer organization is going to let me have a reading group. You know, like I read to the little guys? It is so much fun! I know that sounds silly. You'd have to be there." Her face is glowing like a thousand-watt bulb.

So that's where the glow came from. From Kyle.

"I know, Michelle. You forget. Kyle used to take me out there. And, years before that, my mother used to live out there. So, I am not totally ignorant about the barrio." I can't keep the edge out of my voice.

"Right. Sorry." She is on her feet. "Got to go. Come see me, soon? Give me a ring and we'll plan something, okay?"

"You can't go yet. We just got started. Don't you want to hear about my new guy?" I ask. I am begging and we both know it.

"I can't think of anything I'd rather do, but Kyle is downstairs. Yeah, he's in the front yard waiting with our bikes. We've got to be at the barrio in . . . hey, we're late." She patters to the door. "See you," she says, and is gone.

I drag across the floor like an alligator. I pull up to a window and look out. Just to torture myself. The two happy ones aren't looking where they are going. They are so busy talking to each other, they run their bikes off the driveway. Gales of laughter! They wheel back on the driveway and head off again.

I slump down to the floor and lie there.

Why doesn't it help that I dumped Kyle instead of vice versa? Why isn't it okay for him to be going out with Michelle? What did I expect, a period of mourning before he could bring himself to look at another girl? Yeah. That would have been nice.

Somebody knocks at my door. Dad. He is the only person who ever knocks at doors around here.

"Wait," I call. I jump up and look at myself in the mirror. Sixteen never looked so bad. I go in the bathroom, splash my face and come out.

"Come in," I call.

Judge Wesley Petty, as I live and breathe. Won't you sit down, your honor? What can I do for you? Carve out my liver and serve it on a platter?

I don't say any of that.

"Hello, Dad," I say. I sit on the rug again and point him to a chair. "Have Elaine and Dean come back, yet?" I ask.

He gives his small, neat head of white hair a quick shake. He looks like a skinny beardless

Santa Claus, but look again. Nobody would ever say his blue eyes twinkle. They glitter.

"I haven't seen much of Elaine. She's been here for more than a week and all I see is her coming and going. If I hadn't made it clear that she should be here every night for dinner, I'd never get to see her."

"Aww!" I say. I'm here all day every day. Totally visible.

"Tell me, Emily, do you think she is shy about me? I mean, she isn't trying to avoid me, is she? You would know, so be honest." My father asks me. Asks me! My father doesn't ask for advice.

I am impressed. Are we, my father and I, about to have one of those golden moments? What they call "getting close"? Even though it's about his precious Elaine . . . he came to me, didn't he?

"You see her more than I do. Sleeping in the same room as you do." He stops again. He continues with, "What do you think?"

"I don't think Elaine is shy about anything. Don't you remember, you said you could tell us apart because she is the sassy twin?"

He thinks about it and nods. A smile hovers around his lips.

I sit up. I am liking this one-on-one. I find I have a lot more to say. And he is listening!

"I don't think she is avoiding you, Dad. She's just busy. What can she do? As long as Dean is here, she is going to spend all her time with

him. That's the nature of love." I fall forward
on the rug and put my chin in my hands.

"I guess you're right. When is he leaving, do
you know?"

We both laugh.

He sobers up. "I need to get to know that
child. It haunts me that I have a daughter I
don't know. You two really are different, aren't
you? She seems such a go-getter. It makes you
wonder what she plans to be. She'd do well in
law. She has the grit, the tenacity to make a
brilliant career of it. And I could help her. If
she wanted it." He gets up and goes to the door.
He stops and looks back.

He is looking right at me. The daughter he
has always had. The one he knows so well.

He has never said that I would do well in
law. That I have grit and tenacity. Or that I
could have a brilliant career. When he talked
about what a good lawyer Elaine would be, his
voice grew strong. The way it does in court. His
voice carries all over the room when he gets
interested in what he is saying.

"Tell me when Elaine comes in, will you?"
he asks. "And comb your hair. It looks awful!"
He goes out.

He saw me!

I don't even look when the door opens . . . no
knock this time . . . and Mother comes in.

"Are you all right?" she wants to know. "I
saw Michelle downstairs but I didn't see you

with her." She crouches on the rug beside me and peers into my face.

"I'm sleepy. I think I'll take a nap," I say.

"Oh, then I'd better go." She gets up.

I hold up a hand. "Don't go," I say.

She sits on the rug and runs her hand through my hair.

"So beautiful," she murmurs. "Want me to brush it for you?"

"Please, Mother. I just want you to sit here with me," I say. Do I really? I don't know what I want.

"What's the matter, Emily? Do you want to tell me about it?" she asks.

"Nothing. I hate Dad. That's all," I say.

She smiles. "He's a rascal, isn't he? What's he done now?"

"It's not what he does. It's the way he is. Full of garbage," I say.

Mother looks startled.

"You want to hear?" I ask. I raise my head and park it on my hand. "He has picked out Elaine for his new law partner. Not me. Elaine. He says she has grit and tenacity. He says she's brilliant. It's not that I care, not personally, it's just that it's so unfair. What am I? I'll tell you what . . . to him I'm just a piece of the furniture."

Mother takes my hand and rubs it between hers.

"Your father can be insensitive. But he is not an idiot. I can't believe he would overlook you. . . . If he knew that you wanted a career in law, he'd back you up. Maybe you should talk to him about it."

"A career in law? Are you kidding?" I jerk my hand out of hers.

"Did I miss something? If you don't want a career in law, what are you upset about?" she asks.

"I'm not upset," I wail.

Mother puts her arms around me. She whispers to me, "There, there, dear."

It is a comfort. But I know the minute she leaves my room, I'll feel just as bad as I did before. I think about asking her to bring my dinner up to me but I'm afraid I'll sound like a baby.

She gets up. "Let me fill your jacuzzi with bath water, a nice, hot tub full. How would you like me to add a drop or two of eucalyptus oil? How does that sound?"

She fills the tub. I smell the oil.

When she comes out of the bathroom, I am still flat on the rug.

"I'll get up in a few minutes," I assure her.

"That's my girl. See you at dinner," she says, going out. She leaves the door wide open.

Kay and I love each other. But I know I don't need all the things she does for me. Are we in a rut, or what?

We should stop while we're ahead. Now that I am not her baby anymore, we sometimes seem like friends. That's nice. I wish she would give all that attention to dear old Dad from now on, I tell myself.

But what about me? It's terrible to need somebody. Somebody of your very own. And not have anybody you can count on.

I reach up to an end table and lift the telephone. I ask for Troy.

I just want to hear his voice.

When he comes on the line, he is breathless.

"They are releasing me tomorrow, Emily," he says.

I rise up. "That is perfectly wonderful," I yell.

"It's terrible!" he says. "Have you forgotten how I feel about being back in Oakland? Yes, Oakland. My probation officer is sending me straight to a foster home in Oakland. He might as well send me to the chair. If I go to Oakland . . . there's no way I can avoid the homeboys. No, I didn't tell him this. I've got to work this out my way." He lowers his voice. "I am thinking of running away. I have enough money for bus fare to Mexico. I've got a grandmother in Mexico. I could go there."

My heart sinks. I've lost Kyle, I've lost my twin, my girlfriend, and I've lost Dad. And now, there goes my new guy.

"Don't leave me, Troy," I say.

He goes silent. I do, too. I don't know what I mean. But I know I couldn't bear it if Troy disappeared down in Mexico. Maybe for years and years. Maybe forever.

I stare at the rug. I run my fingers through it. All at once, I know what to say.

"Come here."

"Come there?" he asks.

"Come here. Get on the next bus and come here. I've got the perfect place to hide you. Nobody would ever find you at our old farmhouse." I am thrilled with the idea. It is one of those exactly right kind of ideas. I know it is going to work. Why has he gone silent? "You know you want to be with me. I love you, Troy. Please come."

"Come to Florida?" he asks. "I hadn't thought of that. You've got a place for me to stay?" He thinks some more. I know I have won when he says, "I'll have to think about it, but . . . I love you, too."

Troy rides the next few days on the bus. I meet him at the bus station, incognito, with a bandana tied around my head and dark glasses on my face. This is already so much fun!

We ride double on my bike the three miles to the old farmhouse. The minute we get inside, he takes his backpack off and we go into each other's arms.

We kiss about a million times. He looks so good to me I can't turn him loose. He laughs at me and asks if I will show him around. I walk him over the house with my arm around his waist. I love him so much. For loving me.

Troy loves me, I say to myself, again and again.

We get to the kitchen. I pull a paper sack out of my pocket and put it on the table.

"Supper," I say.

Troy is opposite me, across the table. There is a very small table in this room that Kay says is too small for a kitchen.

I always loved this little house with its little rooms. My father, my stepmother, and I would come out here sometimes to rake leaves and picnic. We would have our sandwich lunch at this very table. We could get a close-together feeling without even trying.

Now, Troy and I sit down. We are still only about two feet apart. We don't start eating. Our hands are busy holding.

"I love this house," I tell Troy. "I was born here. Elaine and I played on this kitchen floor. We had this rag doll, a really ragged thing, we . . ." I stop. "But that's not important. The important thing is that you are here."

"I still can't believe it. When you said come, I didn't think it was a good idea. Running away the first day of probation . . . that's not good. But it's not like I am a wanted criminal. Nobody would care if I went to Mexico and stayed there. And if I go back to San Francisco I will go straight back to Juvenile Hall. The worse they can do is keep me for another term. You know how I feel about that. I would really be relieved."

"I want you to go to Mexico, Troy. I want to go with you. I've been thinking about this all day. There is nothing to keep me here."

"Go with me? You can't do that. Mexican men and women don't travel together unless they are married. I know that sounds old-fashioned, but Mexicans are old-fashioned. I'm afraid the answer is no, Emily." He tightens his hands on mine. "But I'm glad you wanted to."

Troy is not the boldest person I ever knew. This is going to be up to me.

I arch myself over the table and kiss him.

I am sitting down again when I stop in mid-air. Suddenly, I know what to do. Still leaning over the table, I yell, "I've got it!"

I sit down with a thud.

"It's so simple," I say breathlessly. "We'll get married."

The guy looks stunned. I jump up and run around the table. Hanging over him I say, "We'll get married in Mexico! We'll leave tonight!"

Troy is on his feet. He grabs me by the arms.

"You can't do that! You've got a life. You've got great plans. You're going to college some day."

Is he trying to spoil things? He sounds like a parent.

"You said you loved me," I say.

His eyes shimmer at me a moment and then he draws me to his chest.

"You really would marry me, wouldn't you?" he says.

"Any woman in her right mind would marry you, Troy. You are a rare kind of guy. Kyle, a guy I used to know . . . he is so busy thinking about his own good times, he never gives a thought to how I feel. Not that it matters. It's just a for-example. And most guys are like him. But you are different. I don't know why you worry about me. But it just makes me love you more."

A look of doubt crosses his face.

"But Emily, we can't. I don't have enough money to take you to Mexico with me. I've got just enough money left for my own bus fare . . . to wherever I go."

I dump the sandwiches out of the sack. I keep holding the sack upside down. I give it an extra shake and a roll of bills comes out.

Troy's brown eyes get wild. He points at the money.

"Wha . . . what . . . ? Where did you get this?" he asks.

"Don't worry, it's mine. I cashed my savings this morning. I wanted to be ready. Just in case we needed it."

We look across the table at each other. Troy's black curls have fallen over his forehead again. I push them back. At my touch, he pulls away.

"I don't think so, Emily. I don't think you should go anywhere with me. My future is just one big blank."

I put my lips against his ear. "We love each other, Troy. Enough said."

He looks down at me and his eyes turn to slits. Shimmering slits.

"That's why I can't let you follow me around."

We love each other. But we can't be together? There is something wrong with this picture.

"I can decide what I want to do," I tell him. Our eyes lock.

There is nothing to keep me here in Fern. Why can't he accept that?

"Please, Troy, don't disappoint me. I am so sick of this place! I am so sick of Dad! Now that Elaine is here, he has forgotten I exist." I can't help it, my eyes fill with tears.

Troy's eyes widen.

"That's the reason you want to leave?" he asks.

He is maddening.

"No! Of course not! But it wouldn't hurt for Dad to find out how it feels to play second fiddle."

Slowly, Troy draws me to him. I cry against his chest. He lifts my chin and kisses my eyes. Very gently.

I swallow to get rid of the lump in my throat and push away from the guy.

"Now, can we make some plans?" I say. "It's getting late." Without waiting for an answer, I go on. "We will stay at your grandmother's until we can get married. Then we'll get jobs and find a place of our own."

Troy sighs. "You Americans," he says. "Jobs! A place of our own! You are a smart girl, Emily, but you have a lot to learn about Mexico."

I don't understand him. And I am too excited to really listen.

"The first thing I have to do is get back home.

I am due at Dad's almighty dinner table in half an hour. If I'm not there, everybody will be looking for me. But I can pack my backpack and sneak away again after dinner. When Dad finds out it will be too late for him to stop us." The idea sends a chilly thrill down my spine. "Oh, Troy, are you as happy as I am?"

I straighten up. My brains are working a mile a minute.

"I'll call the airport from the house. Yes, the airport," I say. "A bus would be too slow. I'll call a taxi, too, to take us to the airport. That will be expensive but there's no other way." I touch the roll of bills. "Hang on to this, Troy. I'll be back in an hour, no more," I am so excited I can hardly breathe.

At that moment, my twin-sense flickers on. Elaine must be thinking about me. Or . . . is she near? I almost panic at the thought. I trust my twin. But this time . . . she might try to stop me. I'd better hurry before she finds out what Troy and I are going to do.

I kiss my guy one more time.

"Before I go . . . we need something to . . . get engaged with," I say. Neither of us is wearing a ring. "We need to trade something. What have you got?"

"Emily, you're going too fast. I still don't know. . . ." He is looking down. He fumbles in his pockets.

I interrupt him.

"I know. I've got it!" I yank the scarf off my neck. The scarf my dad gave me. That special gift. It meant so much to me. I guess it still does. Otherwise, why am I still wearing it?

"Here," I say, holding the scarf up. For a second, I hesitate. The scarf is beautiful. I can see why Dad always had a special feeling for it. Then I take two corners of it and rip. It tears down the middle in a shiny flash. One half is just long enough to go around Troy's neck. I tie the ends in front. Then I tell him to tie the other half around my neck. There! We have performed what I will always call "the scarf ceremony."

"What do they say in wedding ceremonies?" I ask, trying to remember. "Something like, 'I pledge my troth,' which means 'I promise to be true.' " I smooth the ends of the scarf where his shirt hangs open. "How do you like our engagement scarf?" I ask Troy.

"You are an unusual girl, Emily. So strong. So sure of yourself. I can't help but love you."

I draw back. "You sound like you wish you didn't," I say.

"Maybe what I wish is that you didn't love me," he says.

"That's too deep for me," I say, laughing. I put myself in front of him. Up close. "Can you bear to kiss me once more before I go? I've got to hurry." Outside I can see that the yard is in shadow. The sun is down. And somewhere, Elaine is getting ideas.

As I go down the dirt driveway, I remember that my backpack is at Michelle's house. I lent it to her last summer and never got it back. When I reach the pavement I turn toward her house. Just as I turn the corner, I see something that makes me stare. Then, nervously, I squint through the twilight. Someone is coming this way on a bike. In a big hurry.

It looks like . . .

Quickly, I turn off and park behind a hedge. I watch as the bicyclist goes by. It is Elaine! Going like a speed demon toward the road I just left.

I almost panic again. But, I ask myself, what reason would she have to go to the farmhouse at this time of the day? Absolutely none. She has to be seated by Dad at the dinner table in fifteen minutes.

My heart is pounding. But I calm down. Elaine and I have biked out this way before just for the ride. She'll probably be home soon, and whatever happens, I know my twin will be on my side.

I get back on my bike and go for my backpack.

As fast as I can.

CHAPTER EIGHT
Elaine

My trip to the old farmhouse still has me shaking.

I park Kay's bike and run upstairs to Emily's bedroom. She isn't there. I run downstairs to the dining room. There is Emily. She is sitting primly beside Dad. He is leaning toward her and she is leaning away from him with a scowl on her face.

Everybody stops talking and turns to look at me.

"Sorry I'm late," I say, going to my chair on the other side of Dad. I stand behind it. To my father I say, "I've got to go upstairs a minute. I'll be right back."

"But you just got here," Dad says. I didn't know any dignified father could look like that ... like a little boy who lost his kite in a windstorm. It touches me. I really do love him and I want to get to know him. Now he is saying, "I haven't seen you twenty minutes since you got here."

I feel Emily's eyes on me. I look at her. If

looks could kill I'd be dead. I'm getting sick of her attitude. Every time Dad speaks to me, she has a heart attack. It's so unfair. I am his daughter, too.

"Where is Dean?" Dad asks, looking around.

"He's gone home. It's a long story . . . can I tell you later? Right now, I need to talk to Emily." I turn back to my twin. "Come upstairs with me for just a minute?"

When we get to our bedroom, I look around for her backpack. It's not in sight. Emily comes in behind me and goes to stand near the open closet. Why is she standing way over there?

"Okay, Elaine. What's the big mystery? Why am I up here instead of eating my dinner?" she asks.

I park my hands on my hips. "I just came from the old farmhouse. Does that give you a clue?" I ask.

She rushes at me. For a minute I think she is going to hit me.

"Just now? You just came from there?" she asks in a tight voice. "Have you told anybody that Troy is there?"

"Not yet," I say.

She sags back on the bed. Then she sits forward again.

"Not anybody? You promise?" she asks.

"Not anybody. But I think I should. And I probably will," I say.

Now Emily cocks her head at me as though she is trying to read my mind. "Uh . . . what did he . . . did he tell you about his soccer team?"

"You mean did we talk about sports? Don't you wish!"

Emily ducks her chin down and looks up at me challengingly. "So he has come to see me. What's wrong with that?" she says.

I shake my head.

"I know everything. Troy didn't realize he was telling me," I say. "I got the whole story out of him because he thought I was you. So get real. You can't run off with Troy, you know."

Silence. For once I can't tell what my twin is thinking. She keeps glancing at the closet. She reaches up, once, and straightens the pillow on her side of the bed before she turns back to look at the closet again.

I walk over to the closet. I pull out a bulging backpack.

"You win," she says. "It was a crazy idea."

All the pent-up steam goes out of me. I win? Is it really going to be this easy?

"You mean it?" I cry, and sit beside her on the bed. "Talk about relief! You had me soooo worried. Of course, I knew you'd come to your senses. No way would you run off and get married without telling me." I put an arm across her shoulder. "Thanks, Emily. This is the best Christmas present I could get."

Her head whips around and she stares at me.

"You mean that, don't you?" she says.

"What do you want? Do I have to put it into

song so my story can be told to the world? Let's see. . . ."

I stand up, strut like Elvis, and start to play an imaginary guitar. I guess I am giddy with relief.

I strum this invisible instrument and sing, hunting for words as I go: "Oh, my sister, sweet Juliet, fell in love with Romeo, said she'd marry, all in secret. . . ." I stop and screw up my face as though waiting for genius to strike. Then I finish with, "But she just couldn't go. . . ." I fling my guitar into the air and fall back on the bed, kicking up my heels and whooping.

Why isn't she laughing?

"Aw, come on. You'll be okay. Him, too. Believe me, the guy will be . . ." I start to say "relieved, too" but think better of it. "The guy will be okay, too. Let's go eat."

"You go on. Please, Elaine. I want to be alone a few minutes. Just say I'm not hungry. Will you do that for me?" Her blue eyes plead at me. How can I refuse?

I finish my meal sitting beside my old man. He is full of talk. It is all about court. Ugh. How can anybody live like that? The last thing in the world I want to do is give out rewards and punishments. It sounds like old-fashioned parenthood.

It took forever but at last dinner is over. I go back upstairs to check on my twin. She must be feeling let down.

The minute I get to the door, my stomach does a flip-flop. It is too quiet inside. No music. No bath water running. My twin is always either into music or the tub.

I go in. Emily is not there.

I walk straight over to the closet. The backpack isn't there, either.

She lied to me. And I believed her. Anybody could have seen that she gave in too easily. Anybody but me!

I grab a pillow and bury my face in it. I wish I could stay like this permanently. Hiding. I don't ever want to go downstairs and tell the parents. Pandemonium is going to break loose. And that's not the worst of it. They may not even believe me. I have no way to prove that what I tell them is true. By the time I convince them, Emily could be in a plane over Mexico.

I shove the pillow back in place and start to get up. My hand touches something. A piece of paper. Lying neatly in the place where the pillow was. It is a note from my sister. It reads:

Dear Family:

When you find this, I will be gone. Troy and I are getting married. If you want me to be happy, you won't interfere. I will be in touch in a couple of weeks. Please call Mama and tell her I am okay.

I love you all,
Emily

I drag downstairs. Dad and Kay are still at the table with their heads together over cups of coffee. The lovebirds are just coming out of a kiss. I wait.

Then I shatter their world. I tell all. I hand over the note to prove it. They freeze. Two seconds pass. They go crazy.

They get up, run around the table, and bump into each other. Kay takes charge.

"Here, Wesley," she says, throwing his coat at him. The coat misses by a mile. It falls on the floor and he picks it up. She pulls her own coat out of the closet and can't get her arms in it. He helps her like he would a child, poking her arms down into the sleeves, one at a time.

"We must stay calm," they say to each other.

"Where are you going?" I ask.

I think they had forgotten me. Now, they stop absolutely still and look at me. They are so pathetic. It is obvious they would both be lost without their Emily.

"To the old farmhouse?" Dad asks me.

"Then you'd better hurry. In fact, they may not be there anymore," I say.

Dad grabs Kay's elbow and they charge out of the front door.

What I said is probably true. Troy and Emily have had time to get halfway to the airport in Orlando by now.

But all of a sudden, I decide to go with the parents.

I rush outside. The car is already turning out of the driveway onto the street. I hop on Kay's bike. I think I may reach the old farmhouse about the same time the parents do.

But as I turn into the little rutted road that leads up to it, I see fresh tire tracks and I know they have been and gone. That means Emily is not here. I turn my bike around. And stop. I look at the old farmhouse again. There is not one light on in it, but I have this urge. A very strong urge. I decide to check it out.

I get to the house.

It is almost dark when I walk up on the porch. It is dark inside. When I first go in, I don't see anything.

Then I see Emily.

My sister is crouched in a corner of the couch. Not moving.

Silently, I go and sit beside her.

"He's gone, Elaine. Troy is gone," she says. She says it, but everything about her, her voice, her eyes, the helpless wave of her hand, says she doesn't believe it.

Believe it, I want to say.

In a minute she adds, "The money, too."

This I can't believe. Not the money!

She sees me looking at the table where the roll of bills was.

"It's true," she says. "All of it."

We are quiet for a long time.

Finally she gets up.

"I've got to get back before the parents find my note. They drove in here awhile ago. They could have been out for a ride. I hope they weren't looking for me. If they were . . . my bike was out of sight and the house was dark. Anyway, they drove away again. I am so glad they don't know about all this. . . ."

"But, Emily, they do. That's why they came out here."

She whips around. The whites of her eyes look ghostly in the dark room.

"You ratted on me!" she yells.

"I had to," I say. "I had to do it, Emily." I can feel her shock. It hits me so hard I can't think of the words to explain to her why I had to, but I know I did. What else could I do?

"I can't believe you," she whispers. "I trusted you. I thought . . . I thought you and I would always come through for each other. No matter what." Her words come out in a hiss.

I draw back. I am feeling worse by the minute.

"I get it," she hisses. "You did it to show Dad what a good little girl you are. To show him that you are the best twin. Yeah, I know all about it. He thinks you are the one to follow in his footsteps. Not me. Never once did he tell me I should go into law. How did you sell him on the idea that you'd be good at it? Do you see your name on the office door right under his? That'll be a million laughs! The partners. In injustice." Her breath comes out in little explosions.

While Emily talked I could feel the blood rush to my head. When she stops, I throw my head back and scream like an Indian.

"I've had it!" I scream.

I grab her and shake her. I yell, between shakes, "I've had it with you and your stupid jealousy! Every time I say 'good morning' to Dad, you shoot daggers at me. If he asks me about the weather, you act like we are conspiring to hire a hitman to blow you away. What is the matter with you? Can't you face it . . . that I exist? Sometimes I think you wish I had never come back."

I drop my hands. It is totally dark now. I know Emily is here in front of me. I can tell by the way she is breathing. Kind of like I always imagined a warthog would breathe. Snorty.

"And another thing," I say. "You've got it all wrong about that law-career business. I wouldn't be a lawyer if he paid me." I didn't know I was so mad at my father, but at the moment I feel furious at him. "He says, 'Emily is smart.' " I mimic his tone. " 'I don't worry about Emily,' he says. 'She could do anything. Whatever she wants to study, I'll back her up in it. But you,' he says to me, 'Elaine, I worry about you. Maybe it's just because I don't know much about you yet. But I would like to see you choose a career. If you choose law, I could help you!' He says that like I am some slow learner that needs tutoring. Please tell me how you got it that Dad thinks I am better than you?"

I wait. In a busy silence.

I feel her move closer to me.

"He told you I was smart? Are you sure he said that?" she asks.

Doesn't she know? I can't believe Emily

doesn't know how much Dad dotes on her. I should be the jealous one. But there is a difference. I guess it would be hard to see a brand new sister walk into your father's affections. Yeah, that might be hard.

I don't know why we aren't jealous over Mama. It's the same thing, only reversed. But our mother is always up-front. She exercises a big mouth, just like Emily and I do. The three of us talk about everything. Dad can be a real clam. Most of his feelings are kept deep down. It makes me a little sad for Dad. He is missing a lot.

I feel a hand touch mine.

"I've got something to tell you, Elaine," Emily says. "While I was sitting here alone, I did some thinking. I'm not going to blame Dad for what I was about to do. Running off and getting married was my idea. All mine. But I realized something. Sitting right there on that couch in the dark, I realized that . . . this was after I saw that Troy was gone . . . that I wasn't grieving over Troy. I was unhappy that he left me but . . . I was also relieved. Yeah. Can you believe that?"

"Yes," I say. And hold my breath. What is she leading up to?

"Like I said, I did a lot of thinking."

"What about?" I ask.

"It's hard to explain it." Another long pause. "I'm not sure that I ever wanted to marry Troy. I'm not sure that I ever . . . even loved him. Not enough to marry, anyway." She takes a deep breath and says, "What I realized was I just wanted Dad's attention." She gives me a quick, meek look. She lifts her hands and spreads them out in a helpless way. "I found out how to get our old man's attention before I could walk. Being good didn't do the trick so I would be bad. That always worked. Dad was on me like a bumble bee. And every time I got his attention by doing something he didn't want me to do, I felt like I had won. That's sick, isn't it?"

"Not terminally. No, I don't think that you are in the last stages." I know Emily was never very bad as a child. The way I hear it is that she was always too good to be true. Kay swears she was an angel. It is people like Emily who think any little thing they do that isn't perfect is terrible. But I let that go. What my twin is saying sounds right. "I think the patient is going to live," I pronounce solemnly.

Emily's hand grips my arm. "What I just told you . . . Elaine . . . that was so hard to say. I hate to think about it. That I am that kind of person. Somebody who would use a guy, a sweet guy like Troy, to get Dad's attention. And the worst part is that, at my age, I was still trying to get Dad's attention. I've got to work on that."

"No problem," I tell her. "With me around, you don't stand a chance." I hope she is going to laugh.

I hear a muffled sound. Please, not tears.

"You are hopeless." She laughs. Not much of

a laugh. Sort of an I-give-up wail. I'll settle for that.

"Let's go home," I say. "The parents probably drove all the way to the airport. We'll have to wait until they get back to tell them you aren't missing anymore."

We shuffle through the dirt yard to our bikes and turn on the headlights. We ride side by side down the dirt road.

"Want to hear something gross? I got mad at Dean. He left this afternoon," I say. Funny. That didn't come out as sad as I thought it would. Just medium sad.

"Day after tomorrow is Christmas Eve. Talk about good cheer!" she says.

We are on the pavement. We single-file it home.

Before we turn into the long driveway, we can see that the house is lighted from top to bottom.

We stop and stare. I start off again, but Emily reaches over and grabs my arm.

"Do they think I died?" she asked. "What's going on?"

"You're still missing," I say.

We park the bikes and run up the front steps. Kay meets us at the door. Emily allows her stepmother to hold her. I see my twin kiss Kay on the cheek.

This seems to remind Kay that she is mad at Emily.

She pushes her away and holds her at arms' length.

"No matter what you do, no matter how crazy, you must promise me right now . . . to tell us next time," she says.

We go in. Dad steps forward.

Here it comes, I think. Dad is going to blast Emily. The judge is about to hand down the sentence.

He puts himself in front of Emily and looks up at her.

"You don't have to say anything, my child. I heard what happened. But it's over with." He steps closer to her and says, "All your life, you have been my comfort. Even when you presented problems, just having you gave me comfort. That's what I want to give you now." He holds out his arms and Emily puts her head on her father's chest. As Emily goes into Dad's arms, somebody walks up beside them.

Troy!

Kay sees my look of wonder and says, "We had to drive by the bus station to get on the Orlando freeway." She turns to Emily, who has backed away looking shocked. "I don't know how your father recognized Troy. But he did. He stopped the car and called over, 'You're Troy, aren't you?' Just like that."

Emily and Troy give each other a solemn look. They don't go near each other.

"How did I recognize this young man?" Dad asks, looking at Emily. He touches the rainbow scarf around Troy's neck. "I gave this scarf to your mother. A long time ago." He studies Emily. "The night she left Fern, she left it behind. That's why I wanted you to have it when you went to see her, Emily. Did she recognize it?"

Emily and I exchange looks. My twin-sense says that we both hate to tell him no. Slowly, we shake our heads.

Quickly, Emily adds, "She may have, but she didn't say anything about it."

But we know. Mama didn't even notice it. All the pain attached to that scarf and its memories . . . she left that behind, too. Mama is a person of the present.

My dad carries the past around like a soldier boy carrying a very heavy flag. His roots, his ancestors, the works. He is happy in his second marriage, but he keeps the unhappy memory of the first marriage. It is one of his possessions. All the more reason to admire the guy for what he did tonight. About what Emily had done, he was able to say, "Let's forget it. It's over with." So if he's got a fetish about this scarf, I guess I can handle that.

"I'm sorry I tore it, Dad," Emily says. Fingering the half scarf at her neck, she glances at Troy.

I, too, give Troy a close look. Considering he turned thief, he looks very cool.

"I put your money back in your sandwich bag," he says to Emily. "I hid it under the couch cushion. Okay? When I got to the bus station, I bought a postcard and wrote you where to look." He smiles sheepishly and adds, "You'll get the postcard tomorrow."

He takes the torn scarf off his neck and hands it to her. Emily looks down at it. Suddenly she is crying.

Troy turns to the parents. "I would like to talk to Emily, alone."

At Kay's suggestion Emily leads Troy to the small parlor across the hall. She closes the door behind them. But I don't have to eavesdrop to know what they will say.

I could write the script: Emily will be surprised to hear that, just like her, Troy didn't want to get married. She'll say she still loves him, but . . . and he'll say me too. And they'll say, who knows? Someday . . . And they'll say, let's write, et cetera. Okay, it will be romantic. It will be sad and sweet. They will kiss and make vague promises. They may really hope that someday . . . but tomorrow, they are both going to look around at the world like new people. Not ecstatic but relieved. And I wonder how I got so smart?

Dad is on the telephone. I hear him say "Evita," and realize he is talking to my mother.

"I'll put him on the bus. No, he won't accept airfare. Will you meet him? If you could take him straight to the North California Farm Co-op, he wouldn't have to spend more time at Juvenile Hall. Yes, he wants to do the co-op's bookkeeping and earn enough to go to college. Tell them to call me for a recommendation. This young man is all right, and I'd like to say so to his employers." Dad listens, then he coughs. "Evita, I am glad to hear you are well. Emily enjoyed her stay with you. When she left here, I gave her a certain scarf, a rainbow scarf. . . ." He is interrupted. "Of course, I'll tell her. Good-bye." He sits a minute longer after he hangs up the telephone. Then he glances at me.

"Your mother says to tell Emily not to wear that scarf-thing around her neck. It is unbecoming." He sniffs.

I go to him. I want to sit on his lap and ask for a kiss, but I am a big girl now. I settle for a peck on the top of his head.

CHAPTER NINE
Emily and Elaine

"Is this black, or is it navy blue?" Emily asks Elaine.

The twins are seated in the backyard gazebo. They are surrounded by jars of paint.

Elaine takes the jar Emily is holding and studies it. "It could be blue." She dips the brush in it and paints a dark line down one side of her bare foot. "It's blue," she says.

Emily takes the brush out of her hand and very carefully paints a polka dot on her own foot.

"Gimme," Elaine says. She takes the paint brush and paints another wide stripe down her foot from ankle to toe. She looks up at her twin. She offers the paint brush to her. Emily paints her whole foot navy blue.

"What are you going to wear with it?" Elaine asks in a serious tone.

Emily thinks about it. "I've got a silver and blue wand from when I played Tinkerbell in the third grade."

"Perfect," Elaine says. She picks up a jar of

yellow paint and paints her other foot with it. "This will go with my new vest. You know the one with the yellow and black zigzags?"

"Kay is going to fuss," Emily says.

"We can clean up this mess before she sees it. Oh, you mean when she sees our foot-art?" Elaine raises one foot and admires it.

"She won't like the colors. They aren't Christmasy," Emily says.

"I can fix that," her twin says. "Give me the red and green." She takes the jars Emily hands to her, raises a foot, and goes to work.

It is Christmas Eve. The twins are supposed to be getting ready to go with the parents to the community sing uptown. Everybody in Fern will crowd into the square around the bandstand, and Kay will lead the Christmas carols.

"I can't go yet, Elaine. I need to talk about yesterday," Emily says. "I felt bad when Troy left."

"Bad that he's gone . . . or what?"

"Not that he's gone." Emily thinks about it. "I could tell that Troy was ready to leave. He couldn't wait to get to the farm co-op." She turns her head slowly and looks at her twin. "What I felt bad about was the way I used him. I pressured him from the first. I didn't try to get to know him. I still don't know him. Was I a nerd to think he was different from the other first offenders?"

"The Southern Princess lives!" Elaine says, scowling at Emily. "You were a nerd to think those first offenders were all that different from you and me. Especially you." Elaine's voice is edged with disgust. "Didn't you just tell me you didn't try to get to know Troy? That you used him? What's worse than using a person to get what you want? It's like stealing. No, it is stealing. Not just money. Something more important. It's like stealing somebody's trust."

The girls look at each other for a long moment. Emily's chin is tucked in and her eyes are wide. Elaine is rigid.

"It's scary, isn't it?" Emily says at last. "A person can do things and not even know she's doing them. It's scary to think I could kid myself like that. It's like part of me was making all these plans about Troy and the other part was sitting waiting for it to take effect on Dad. It was like the two parts didn't get together."

"Tell me about it," Elaine says, relaxing. "In a way I did the same thing with Dean. I wanted to love him, just so I could be in love. I can remember thinking I would get to know him later. I guess I used him, too, didn't I?" She stops and frowns. "But Emily, when it comes to users, Dean makes you and me look like amateurs. I thought Dean was the smoothest, coolest, most polite guy I ever saw. I thought, there goes a guy who is headed for big things. He's got all the right moves. He never says anything dumb. I mean, later you realize what he says is dumb, but you don't know that at the time. He could talk a polar bear into buying a fur coat. And make it sound like he's doing the bear a favor. And the bear . . ."

Emily interrupts Elaine.

"You can use your own name. You don't have to call yourself a polar bear. But wait. The way you told me about this . . . you didn't buy the fur coat."

"No. But I felt so stupid. He made me look bad, Emily. He has a way of making himself right and the other person wrong. He can confuse me in a minute."

"But you're okay now? You're going to get over him?" Emily asks.

"Maybe," Elaine says, "but I hurt. I lost my one and only."

"And I lost mine," Emily says.

The girls begin to put the lids back on the paint jars.

"It's going to get pretty lonesome," Elaine says.

Emily stops and touches her twin on the shoulder, turning her toward her. "I wish you weren't going back next week."

"Me, too," Elaine says. "Better still, I wish you were coming to California with me. We could paint our feet and . . . you know what we could do? We could give a foot-painting party. Make everybody take their shoes off and . . ."

"Give prizes, but don't let anybody get a prize for painting their feet plain skin-colored. . . ."

"We could have stick-on designs and sequins and . . ."

"What about hands? Do we paint hands, too?"

The girls think about it.

"Elaine, we can't do this. We both have to go back to school." After a second, Emily adds, "But what about spring break? You have to come back then."

Elaine bends toward Emily. "I like it. Let's get new bathing suits. Something devastating Suits the color of watermelons and paint our feet to match, okay?"

Emily rises up on her knees. "No, let's get skin-colored suits and paint our feet green."

"Or one green and one plain." Elaine says. "My left foot and your right foot, both green. The other feet not painted, okay?"

"Deal." Elaine and her twin pump their hands in a politician handshake, up and down.

"Daytona Beach will never be the same," Emily promises Elaine. "Hold that thought. Now, let's go get dressed."

Elaine jumps to her feet, pounds her chest, and yells, "Listen up, guys, wherever you are. Spring breaks may come and go, but this one will be different because . . ."

Emily jumps up beside her and sings out, "The redheads are coming!"

About the Author

Charlotte St. John is a professional illustrator as well as a writer, with Masters degrees in both Art and Psychology. A native Floridian, she and her husband currently live in a Vermont-like house in a Florida swamp. They have three children. RED HAIR, TOO is the author's fourth novel, following SHOWDOWN, FINDING YOU, and RED HAIR.

Eat Your Heart Out in the
HEARTBREAK CAFE

FOR GIRLS ONLY

by: Janet Quin Harkin